Crossing the Line 2:

A Chaotic Love

A Novel By

Dejah Rice

Text **ROYALTY** to **42828** to

join our mailing list!

To submit a manuscript for our review, email

us at submissions@royaltypublishinghouse.com

Text RPHCHRISTIAN to 22828

for our CHRISTIAN ROMANCE novels!

Text RPHROMANCE to 22828
for our INTERRACIAL ROMANCE novels!

LEGAL NOTES

© 2016

Published by Royalty Publishing House

http://www.royaltypublishinghouse.com

CHAPTER 1

CASANOVA

A few weeks had passed by and things were kosher. Only thing I hated was that Elle was back home with Charles now. That spoiled fucking brat was messing up everything for me. Charles wasn't as available as he was when she was gone. I mean, yeah, he was still sending me money, but I wanted more than that from him.

I wanted his time and attention. I needed to feel his smooth lips on my skin and his firm hands on my ass. That man did my body wonders. Now I felt deprived and I wasn't feeling that at all. Yes, Sean would break me off some dick, but he had always pretty much been the weakest link in that area. Since Rio wasn't filling that void anymore, Charles was definitely it. I loved my money and my money loved me, but I needed more at times. Especially when it came to that sexy ass Charles.

Speaking of Rio though, I hadn't heard from him since that night. He didn't send me any texts and he didn't call either. He had basically gone ghost on me. I can't complain about that though. Him disappearing was exactly what I needed. Especially if I planned on keeping things good with Sean, which I did. He wasn't the best lover, but he was definitely the best supplier and I needed that. *Mama didn't raise a fool!*

"Have you heard from that guy?" I asked London. We were in

the nail salon getting pedicures since it was Friday and we didn't have shit else to do.

"What guy?" she asked, texting away on her phone.

"Rio's friend!" I snapped.

"Oh, him! Nope, haven't heard one thing from him. But you know how I do my business. I already have a man, so after the job is done, I don't keep in touch, unless they plan on doing business again."

"Mmm."

"I still can't get over dinner that night! Sean sat down and was like 'what you doing with my girlfriend?' Bitch, I could have died!"

"Darling, you? I wanted to disappear. I was clicking my heels together underneath the table and all!"

"That's so fucking funny."

"Yeah, now it is," I said, getting up after our toes had dried. We paid and tipped the folks who'd done our feet before heading out.

"What's up, baby?" I heard a male ask as soon as we had walked out of the shop. I looked over and saw a dark-skinned guy with dreads coming out of the subway beside the nail salon.

"Hey, Gutta!" London yelled, smiling big as hell.

"Who is that?" I hissed while squinting my eyes.

"That's Gutta. Your sister boyfriend's homeboy," she explained.

"Oh, you know I don't be knowing anybody," I laughed as the guy came face to face with us.

"What's up, Lon?" he asked.

"Not much, honey. Where that loud at though?" London asked, and I sucked my teeth while rolling my eyes hard as fuck. Smoking was just so nasty to me. Females getting high period was repugnant.

"You know I got you! Why don't you come take a ride with me? Know I'll match you," he said.

"Match her?" I blurted out. I didn't have the slightest idea about what they were talking about.

"Yeah, ma, meaning we both roll something up and smoke together," he explained, chuckling.

"Oh," I said uninterested again.

"You look familiar, shawty," he said, rubbing his goatee.

"This is Harmony's big sister, Gutta," London said. He instantly looked pissed as soon as the name Harmony left her mouth.

"Word, what's ya name, ma?" he asked eyeing me.

"It's Casanova, but you can call me Nova."

"Ms. Nova, do me a favor?" he asked.

"What kind of favor?" I asked with my nose turned up.

"I need you to give your sister something for me."

"What is it?"

"Something small, nothing major."

"Okay, I guess I can give it to—"

WHAP!

He backhanded me before I could even finish talking, causing me to fall to the ground. I saw red and quickly hopped up off the ground. I started digging through my purse ferociously. He continued to stand there with his hand reared back. If I didn't know any better, I would think he wanted to hit me again. Too bad it wasn't going to be today. I found my pepper spray and snatched it out of my purse.

"WHAT THE FUCK IS YOUR PROBLEM?!" I yelled as I sprayed him in the eyes with the pepper spray. He immediately hollered out like a little girl.

"That's enough, Nova!" London yelled while trying to drag me away. I had stopped spraying him in the eyes, but I still stood there pissed.

"Better get your girl out of here, London, before it's too late. Ay, ma, don't forget to give your bitch ass sister that for me!" Gutta yelled and smirked as he held on to his eyes. I lunged at him, but before I could hit him, London successfully pulled me away.

"What was his problem?" I asked London angrily.

"I don't know, sweetie. Sorry about that. Are you okay?"

"I'm fine," I said as we both hopped in my car. I don't know what that guy's problem was, but Mony would definitely be hearing from me. I don't care if we were pissed with each other or not. Her problems had approached me and I didn't like that one bit! "How do you even know him?" I questioned.

"Like I said, he's cool with Mony's boyfriend and you know they be getting that money, right?"

"Yeah, and?"

"My brother wanted to link up with them a little while ago, so I called up Mony to see if they would put him on. They agreed to it, so I took my brother over to Mony's apartment. When we went, I met AK and Gutta. Ever since then, I've been shopping with Gutta whenever my brother's not around," she explained.

"Shopping with him?"

"Getting weed from him. Damn, Nova," she said laughing.

"Bitch, I didn't know!"

"Well, you do now."

Once we were in my car, I connected my phone to the Bluetooth system for my stereo. I had just started getting into the song when my phone started ringing. I saw it was Charles calling and immediately answered it. Since my phone was already connected to the stereo, I decided to just talk to him without disconnecting my phone. London saw his name on my phone and started eyeing me suspiciously.

"Hey, Charles, how are you?" I asked sweetly.

"I'm good. I just got off of work and Elle just called and said she had something to handle after school. Think you can come over for a quickie? I got a couple of stacks for you," he said, causing me to gasp. I quickly disconnected my phone from the Bluetooth system and turned my stereo down. I knew London heard him though, and it was too late. I don't even know why I took the call around her. It was that damn Charles! I couldn't think straight when it came to him.

"I have to call you back!" I yelled into the phone and hung up.

"Bitch, I know you not fucking your baby sister's nigga?!"

"She's not a damn baby, so mind your fucking business! I'm all about money just like you, so please don't try to judge me because you're no better!" I yelled, trying to make it seem like I was only trying to get paid. Which was true in the beginning.

"I do have some kind of morals though, Nova. I would never fuck with my sibling's mate. That shit is just low!" she scolded.

"What the fuck ever! Just keep your mouth closed."

"I don't know if I can do that."

"You know what, get the fuck out!" I yelled and pulled over.

"Gladly, bitch! Just know I will be telling Mony about this so she can let Elle know how you really rock!" she yelled, before hopping out of my car and taking off down the street. *Stupid bitch!*

I finally made it home after kicking London out of my car. The audacity of that girl! She was supposed to be my best friend, but what kind of best friend snitches on you? I don't care what you've done, that's just not right. But, then again, who was I to look for loyalty? Who needed loyalty anyways when there was money to be made. I must admit that I enjoyed Charles outside of the money thing though. I was really starting to get into him before Elle returned home.

It was early in the evening and I was about to relax. I walked in my front door and headed straight upstairs. After I was done

11

freshening up, I walked back down the stairs and joined Sean in the living room with a glass of wine. We were laughing at the TV when we heard a doorbell ring. Well, Sean was laughing... I was fake laughing. I was still pissed about the shit that had happened with London.

"I got it," Sean said and headed to the door. He repeatedly asked who it was just to get no answer in return. "Who the fuck is it?!" he yelled out, aggravated, as he snatched the door wide open. His face dropped as the visitor pushed his way inside of our home.

"YOU LET THIS NIGGA KNOW THAT WE WAS FUCKING YET AND THAT YOU WAS MY BITCH?" Rio asked, heading straight for me with fire in his eyes. I could tell that he was drunk by the way he stumbled towards me.

"Nova, what the hell is this dude talking about?" Sean asked looking at both of us. The real question was how had Rio found out where I stayed at. I opened my mouth to respond, but nothing was coming out. *Shit!*

"Speak the fuck up! You must have thought that I was just gone let you ride off into the sunset with this nigga! Hell nah, not after the way you broke my heart!" Rio yelled, pissing me off.

"Nova!" Sean yelled. I guess he wanted answers immediately and he was about to get them too! I scrunched up my face trying to make some tears come. When I felt one slowly roll down my cheek, I knew it was game time.

"I don't even know this crazy man like that, baby. He's trying to ruin us! I want him out of our house and I don't think you should do business with him either!" I yelled, crying hysterically.

"Okay, Nova, calm down. Sir, we both would appreciate if you would leave our home. I no longer will be able to do business with you, but I wish you the best of luck," Sean said as he placed his hand on Rio's arm, trying to get him to leave.

"Get the fuck off of me! Sucker duck ass nigga! Can't you see this bitch lying? She's been playing both of us! If I ain't know her, how do I know she got a rose tatted on her left ass cheek?" Rio questioned.

"Damn it! Come clean right now!" Sean said, staring me down.

"He only knows that because I told him at dinner that night," I said as I continued to cry.

"Bitch, you lying!" Rio yelled at me before turning his attention back to Sean. "Fuck all of that dawg. Look, I pay for her to stay in a condo not too far away from here. I bet she was getting a kick out of that shit being that you got her staying in this mini mansion and shit. If you don't believe me, meet me over there Monday morning and I can show you!"

"Okay, okay, damn!" I yelled, fed up. I was busted and my

little game was over. "What he is saying is true, but I don't want him, Sean. I want you!"

"Why you always lying?!" Rio blurted out and I shot him a look.

"Why the fuck you still in my house? Matter of fact, how did you know where I live at?" I asked bothered.

"I got it from ya dude's partner. Called him up and he gave it right to me," Rio said cockily.

"I can't believe you, Nova," Sean said, looking hurt. "I can never… forgive you… for… this," he said all dramatic and shit.

"Y'all know what? To hell with the both of you because Nova gone be alright!" I yelled, and made my way up the stairs to pack my shit and plan my next move. They both remained standing in the middle of the floor, looking at each other like some fools.

After I was done packing some of my shit, I headed down the stairs. When I got downstairs, the house appeared to be empty. I held on to my shit as I made my way out of the house. Once I was outside, I noticed that my car was the only one in the driveway. I was relieved. Fussing with those niggas some more was not the way I wanted to end my night.

I guess Rio was satisfied with the way things went and left. Then, there was Sean who was probably fucking heartbroken. Like

I said before, to hell with the both of them. I don't have pizazz, a killer strut, and this angelic face for nothing! All of that could get me only so far though. Even though it always took me pretty damn far. But, I had something more, and that something more was brains.

I may have lost this round with the two of them, but that just meant I could really keep my eyes on the prize now. I hopped in my car after putting the things I had packed in my back seat. I sat there for a moment and thought of my next move. A hotel was out of the question for me, I just wasn't feeling that. But, I did have something up my sleeve.

I reached in my back seat and pulled my cell phone out of my bag. I put on my game face as I slowly dialed a number. This was going to have to work or I would be forced to come up with something else. It was late now, and I really didn't have time for that. I needed to get this move into play right away. The sooner the better. Well, that's what they say and I couldn't say I disagreed.

CHAPTER 2

NOELLE

Today was Friday and I dreaded going to class. Things with Professor Black and I definitely weren't good. I can't believe I had allowed things to go as far as they did with him. Now, he had things over my head that I never wanted anyone to find out. These things needed to remain as my terrible little secret.

I just wanted to forget about it all, but he was making that very hard for me to do. He would glare at me the whole class period. He continued to make me sit right at the front. That wasn't even the worst part. The worst part is that he had actually started flunking me.

I know he is just pissed because I have been refusing to meet him in his office after class. I also have been ignoring all of his phone calls and creepy texts. That's no reason to fail me though. It was close to the end of the semester and I needed to pass, or I would be forced to take summer classes. Summer classes were out of the question for me because I wanted to find a job so that I could make some money of my own. I was sick of depending on Charles and my dad.

Things with Charles and I had only been going okay. Charles was very tentative my first week back home. That only lasted for that week though. After that, he was back to hardworking Charles, which I didn't have a problem with. What I had a problem with was him never admitting to his wrongs.

He also had started laying his phone face down whenever he was around me. He had never done that before, so I knew he was hiding something. That's why I was making him sleep in one of the guest rooms. He swore I was overreacting, but we both knew that wasn't the truth. That's why he went to the guest room without a fuss or fight.

I often cried myself to sleep. I couldn't catch a break or be happy with the way things were going at school and at home. I had nobody to talk to and that hurt the most. Harmony wasn't speaking to me much after I had stood her up. She would text me every other day with some encouraging words, but that was about it.

I didn't mean to stand her up, I had just got caught up with the professor that day. I couldn't blame her for being mad though, and I didn't even bother reaching out to Nova. Nova was a real ice queen. I realized that about her a long time ago. I still loved my sisters though and nothing could change that.

After I was done getting ready for school, I headed to the kitchen where I found Charles at. He was munching on a piece of toast and texting away on his phone. He was so occupied with that darn phone that he hadn't even noticed me yet. I walked further into the kitchen just to still go unnoticed. I cleared my throat loudly and glared at him.

"Oh, hey, Elle… I didn't see you standing there," he said as he placed his phone down on the counter beside him. Face down, of course.

"I know you didn't," I mumbled, as I looked away from him and headed to the refrigerator for some orange juice.

"Did you need something?" he asked, looking bothered.

"No."

"Well, I thought you did. You were clearing your throat loudly like you needed something."

"I don't need anything from you, Charles."

"Sure you do."

"You're right… I do."

"I knew it," he said.

"The truth."

"Huh?"

"I need the truth."

"Elle, please don't start with that."

"Why not? You asked me if I needed something so I'm telling you what I need."

"I'm going to be late for work," Charles said, dismissing me. He finished up his toast and downed a bottle of water before grabbing his phone and heading out of the kitchen. He wasn't even due at work for another hour. I didn't say anything though. I just watched him gather his stuff and leave. I knew he was only trying to avoid having that conversation with me. He always did.

I made myself breakfast and relaxed for a little bit before heading to school. Once I got to school, I headed straight to the class I dreaded going to. Bad thing is I had been dreading this class one too many times this semester. I needed for things to change and quick. With the way things were going though, I would be visiting that bag of cocaine in my bottom drawer sooner than later.

I should have just flushed it, but I'm glad I didn't. I didn't know how much longer I would be able to remain strong in my storm. That cocaine definitely looked like the light at the end of the tunnel right about now. I was glad to have it, but I would try to stay clear from it for as long as possible. No matter how great doing it would make me feel.

Class went by slow, of course. The professor glared at me like usual and I couldn't focus for anything. He kept jumping off of topic, and I didn't like that at all. I think he knew I didn't like it too. I'm pretty sure the expression on my face gave it all away. That's probably why he continued to do it, just so he could mess with me.

After the professor's class, I decided to go to the library on campus. I really needed to study, even though I felt like it didn't matter since he was purposely failing me. I still wanted to prepare myself, though. It wouldn't be right to slack off just because of him and his messed up ways.

Before I knew it, a couple of hours had passed by and it was well into the evening now. I stood and packed my things so that I could leave. The whole time I was studying, I couldn't get the professor off of my mind. That's why I decided to stop by his office before I went home. I just prayed he would still be in there. I really hoped we could come to an understanding about things because my failing grade in his class just wasn't sitting right with me.

I called Charles on my way to the professor's office, to let him know I had something to handle. He had just gotten off of work himself. He probably wouldn't do anything, but go home and sip on some Jack Daniel's and text his mistress. He didn't know this, but if he didn't tighten up and soon, I was going to be leaving him. That's why I needed to pass this class so I would be able to get a summer job.

Yes, I had money, but once I left I would be leaving Charles his money. I didn't want or need it. I would keep the money I got from my daddy, but it would only last so long. I could get more from him, but I was really trying to grow up. Nova constantly called me a spoiled brat and I was sick of that.

When I made it the professor's office, his door was closed. I started to walk right past it, but I decided to at least knock to see if he was in there. I knocked on the door and it came swinging open seconds later. Professor Black stood at his door eyeing me for what felt like forever, before a smile blessed his face.

"Hey…umm… are you busy? I wanted to talk to you… but if you're busy… I can umm… go," I said rambling.

"I'm never too busy for you, Ms. Banks. Come on in and close the door behind you," he said, before walking off and taking a seat behind his desk. I made my way into his office and closed his door like he had asked. I took a seat in one of the chairs in front of his desk.

"So, I umm… really needed to speak with you."

"Then speak."

"I wanted to ask why I was failing your class all of a sudden."

"I was wondering the same thing."

"What do you mean?"

"I mean I've noticed a drastic change in your work. It's not consistent and unfortunately, your answers on the tests we have been having just haven't been right."

"I'm a very consistent person when it comes to my school work! I spend hours studying every day… even on the weekends! So please cut the shit and tell me why you're failing me, professor!" I snapped. I hadn't meant to, but I was passionate about my school work. The way he had sat there and lied and talked down on my work had infuriated me.

"It's Curtis, remember," he said casually, like we were out having tea or something.

"Please, answer my question."

"You already know the answer to your question."

"I want the real answer!"

"Ah, I see. The real answer is you've been ignoring my phone calls and texts. You refused to come see me in my office and most importantly, you shut me out after finally letting me in. We had an amazing night, if I do say so myself. I want to relive that night over and over again, but I can't! You refused to see me or talk to me outside of class! I didn't like that one bit, Ms. Banks! So what do I do? I FAIL YOUR FUCKING ASS AND MAKE YOU COME CRAWLING TO ME!" he yelled, as he suddenly started to look deranged.

"I think I'm going to go."

"SIT THE FUCK DOWN!" He banged on his desk as he stood

up. I eased back down in my seat and stared at this man with fear in my eyes. "You look so beautiful today, Noelle," he said calmer, after seconds of silence had passed by. I hadn't noticed this before, but the professor was crazy.

"Umm, thank you."

"Why did you do this to me, huh?"

"Do what?"

"You lured me to you just to shut me out. I don't like being shut out. You let me make love to you and you loved it. Don't be like her, Noelle. Don't up and leave me! I CAN'T TAKE THIS SHIT AGAIN!"

"Wh—what are you talking about?"

"My ex-wife… she left me. She took my daughter and left me. After five long years! I won't allow that to happen with us."

"What are you talking about?" I asked again, my voice trembling.

"When I want something, baby, I get it. When I get it I become obsessed with it," he explained like he was saying something normal.

"You need help."

"No, I need you and I'm going to have you. Right after we do some lines of cocaine, of course."

"I can't!"

"You will! You said you would always be my freaky girl, now bring her out!" he yelled, as he pulled a baggie full of cocaine out of his drawer. He quickly made two lines in front of me and set a straw down beside it. "Go ahead," he urged.

"No."

"Yes! Now do it before you really piss me off and I flunk your ass for real!"

"Please don't make me," I cried.

"DO IT NOW!" he yelled and I picked up the straw. Maybe if I did it I could get out of here without him attacking me. I placed the straw up my nose and began to sniff.

"Professor Black, I need you to…" someone barged into his office and said, but stopped when they saw me. I could only imagine what was going through this person's head. I dropped the straw and fell to the ground. *What am I going to do?!*

"GET OUT NOW! WHY WOULD YOU JUST BARGE INTO MY OFFICE WITHOUT KNOCKING?! GO, AND FORGET WHAT YOU SAW IN HERE OR I'LL RUIN YOU!" the professor yelled, looking pissed.

The person said sorry a million times before finally leaving and closing the door. I continued to lay on the floor and cry. The professor ignored me as he did the two lines that were on the desk. When he was finished, he stood up and pulled me off of the ground. Then he placed me back into the chair I was sitting in before.

"How are you feeling?" he asked as I cleaned my face with a tissue I had gotten off of his desk.

"What do you care? I'm going home," I mumbled. I was fed up.

"You can go home, Noelle. But, this thing with us is far from over. You should feel lucky that we were interrupted. I'm not in the mood to continue our fun now. See you Monday... my nasty girl," he said and winked at me. I threw up in my mouth and quickly swallowed it back down, as I made my way out of his office.

I didn't even have his class on Mondays so he would not be seeing me. It would be a blessing if I made it to school period. There was nothing that could be done about him, being that the dean was his sister-in-law. I could go to the police, but I felt like I would be dragged down with him. If my daddy ever found out about this, he would lose his mind and probably go to his grave early! I just had to handle this on my own and keep this whole thing to myself.

I hopped in my car and headed straight to the park. I didn't get out or anything, I just sat there and cried for a little bit. A few hours had passed by, by the time I was able to pull myself together. I wiped my face one last time before heading on home. When I finally got home, it was late and dark.

I grabbed my things, got out the car and headed inside. I went straight to my bedroom to put my things down. When I came back to the living room, I noticed Charles sitting on the couch. He was going over some papers and not paying much attention to his surroundings. I turned on the TV and found some cartoons to watch.

I was interrupted by my stomach growling repeatedly. Before I could do anything about it, my phone started ringing. The name that appeared across my screen had me surprised. It was my sister, and I'm not talking about Harmony either. I inhaled deeply before answering the phone.

"Hello?"

"Sister! I'm so glad you answered," Nova said into the phone quickly. It sounded like she had been crying.

"Oh my gosh! Casanova, is something wrong?" I asked, worried about her. Who am I kidding though. Something had to be wrong if she was calling me. I loved her, but I knew I wasn't her favorite person.

"Yes, it is! I need you, Elle," she said sniffing. The tone of her voice alone had me wanting to cry.

"What do you need, Nova?"

"I'm afraid to ask."

"Whatever you need the answer is yes."

"Really, Elle?"

"Yes, now what can I help you with and what's the matter?" I asked eagerly, ready to be there for my sister.

"Sean and I got into it… bad. I don't won't to say anything more on that."

"Trust me, I understand! You wouldn't believe what I've been going through."

"Umm, yeah, about that favor though," she said getting back to the point.

"I'm sorry, Nova. What did you need?"

"I need somewhere to stay. I don't want to go to a hotel… I would be so lonely. I want to be around my family right now. I would have asked Harmony, but you know she stays in the hood," Nova said talking very fast.

"Nova, slow down. I told you the answer was yes to whatever you needed. I'm sure Charles won't have a problem with you staying here." Charles shot me a funny look, but I ignored him and continued talking. "You know what? I'm not even going to ask him. You're my sister, so come on over when you're ready and you can stay as long as you need."

"Really?! That's fantastic! I'll be over right away!" she said excitedly before hanging up the phone. The sadness had left her voice and all.

"What was that about?" Charles asked, as he set the papers he was looking over down on the couch beside him.

"Nova needs a place to stay. I told her she could stay with us."

"You did what? Elle, why would you do that without talking to me first?!" Charles looked like he was close to losing his mind. I knew exactly why too, and I was about to call him out on his foolery.

"You heard me talking to her on the phone, Charles! Why are you so upset? Oh, wait, I know. I bet it's because you won't be able to fool around with your mistress anymore now that two sets of eyes will be on you!" I yelled, breathing hard. I was glad Nova was coming to stay. This is exactly what I needed. My sister staying here with me was going to be the best thing ever!

"I'm going to bed," he said before standing up and gathering his papers. After he had everything, he stomped down the stairs.

"Good night!" I yelled out as I made my way into the kitchen.

It was late and I was starving, so I pulled a couple of pots and pans out and made myself some Shrimp Alfredo. I had just sat down to eat when I heard my doorbell ringing back to back. I hopped up out of my chair and made my way to the front door. I opened the door up and there stood Nova. I thought she would have looked a mess after the way she sounded on the phone. But nope. She stood there looking like her normal beautiful self.

"Come on in," I said and smiled politely. I figured she was just trying to hold herself together in front of me. She hated letting people see her at her weakest moments.

"I really appreciate this, Elle," she said as she walked into the house with one bag and her purse.

"Where's the rest of your things?"

"I'll have to get them later. I just grabbed whatever to last me for a few days."

"Okay, well I know you haven't really been over to my place that much, so follow me and I'll show you where you will be sleeping," I said, as I led her downstairs. I walked her to the room across from the one where Charles was at. Once we got in front of the room door, she stopped and looked over at the room Charles was in.

"Is someone in there?" she asked. The light was on and you could see it shining underneath the door.

"Yes, that's just Charles... we have been... umm... having a couple of problems. So, he has been... umm... sleeping down here," I explained as I stared at the floor. I didn't know if she was aware of the problems between us or not, and I really didn't feel like going into detail at the moment.

"Well, I applaud y'all. At least you're able to stay in the same house and you're trying to get it right," she said and cocked an eyebrow. Although she said it as a statement, I felt like it was more of a question.

"Umm, yeah," I said and made my way on into the room. I turned on the lights and looked around to make sure everything was okay for my sister.

"This is a cute little room."

"Thanks. You could have stayed in the master bedroom down here, but like I said, Charles is occupying it right now."

"No, it's fine. I'm just glad you guys are trying to work through your problems," she said and smiled genuinely. But for some reason that smile didn't quite reach her eyes. Her eyes said something else. I just couldn't read them.

"Thanks. I know it's late, but I cooked if you're hungry."

"I'm good. I'm going to get settled in and then I'm going to go to bed after I shower."

"Alright, well there are towels and things in the closet in the bathroom. I won't be back down tonight so if you need anything, don't hesitate to ask Charles."

"Sure won't," she said, smiling brightly.

I told her goodnight and headed back upstairs to eat. My food was cold by now so I had to reheat it. It was still very delicious though. After I finished eating, I put the rest of the food in the fridge. I placed the dishes in the dishwasher and turned it on. Then I headed to the bathroom in my room and ran myself a bubble bath. It had been a long Friday and I needed to unwind.

CHAPTER 3

HARMONY

I was at my place, kicking it with this girl named Hazel. She lived across the hall from me and had gone to school with me in the past. We used to kick it every now and then, and she was a real down ass female. I had been chilling with her a lot lately and she was cool as hell.

Hazel had light skin that kind of resembled butter cream. She had natural, wavy, jet black hair that was cut into a bob. Her eyes were the color of honey. She was a little bit on the chunky side but she wore it well, and her confidence was out of this world. I never hung with her a lot before because I kept my circle small.

I would only deal with so many people at a time. Now that I wasn't fucking with Nadia and I wasn't on the best of terms with my sisters like that, I could really get to know her. I wasn't the type of person to say fuck everybody after shit had gone down. I gave everybody a fair chance with me. But once you crossed that line, that was it, and Nadia had done that.

Therefore, I was done with her flawed ass. I was too much of a solid bitch to be hanging with her anyway. Thing is, I've always known that. But that was my girl so I rocked with her. *Lesson learned!*

"I still can't believe Nadia did you like that. That's some hoe ass shit for real, dawg. Best believe if I see her, I'm running all the way up in her shit! I've been itching to beat a bitch's ass too!" Hazel said, as she constantly kept slapping her fist in the palm of her hand. I was laughing like hell. This girl was just as crazy as me.

"Bitch, and call me first so I can come fuck some shit up too!"

"Okaaayyyy!"

"Oh my God, I wish AK would stop calling me," I complained, as my phone started ringing for the millionth time.

"The fuck does he want?"

"I don't even know, but I'm about to shoot his ass a text!"

Me: Stop texting my fucking phone dude!

Akeem: Chill it ain't even nothing like that.

Me: What the fuck you want then?

Akeem: I want you to make one last run for me at ten!

Me: Nigga hell to the no! Gone head!

Akeem: Stop playing Mony. I need you tonight… the guy that usually goes been fucking up lately. I'm trying to see if it's something going on or is it just him.

Akeem: I'm willing to pay extra!

I set the phone down and took a breath. I was straight when it came to money, but I was never one to deny a dollar bill. Then, he wanted to pay me extra. Oh, hell yeah. I was going to make this move tonight. But once I was done I was going to change my number.

AK was not good with me! Bitches loved cutting off the female, but they still would continue to fuck with the no good nigga. That was that bullshit and it proved how ignorant females could really be over a nigga. Nope, not I, because everybody got cut off when it came to me. Bitches needed some get right in these streets.

Me: That's a bet! I'll get on the interstate at ten.

Akeem: Good looking out, baby.

Akeem: For real!

Akeem: You know I miss you... maybe after you get back you can slide through?

Me: Nigga, bye!

"Girl, niggas be so thirsty," I said laughing, as I set my phone down on the couch beside me.

"What he said?"

"Some bullshit. But look, I'm about to take a nap so I'm going to get up with you later."

"Okay, just hit me up. I need to get back over here to my baby's father anyway. I know him and that little girl of mine probably done tore my damn apartment down."

I let Hazel out of my apartment and went and laid on the couch. I really liked Hazel; she was just that bitch, if you asked me. She was understanding and she didn't try to get all in my business. She was cool with whatever I told her and didn't try to find out more than what she was told. She was a solid bitch like me and I definitely could see us hanging out even more.

***

I woke up to my alarm on my phone going off. I turned my alarm off and saw that it was 10 on the dot. I hopped up and got in the shower. When I got out, I threw on some jogging pants with a t-shirt and pulled my hair up into a bun on the top of my head. I slid on my Nike sandals and grabbed my keys, phone, and purse before heading out the door.

When I made it to the bottom of the stairs, I saw Carrie coming out of the apartment beside hers. This would be my first time seeing her since I had been staying here, and I had been here for weeks. I rolled my eyes and walked right past her. One, because I was running late. Two, because I wasn't in the mood to try to fight her messy ass.

"So, you just gone walk past a bitch like you don't see me?" I heard her say. I turned around so fucking fast. Like bitch, don't speak to me!

"Damn, I thought all peasants knew to only speak when they have been spoken to," I said smirking.

"Kind of like you just did... huh?"

"Girl, if you don't take your broke back mountain ass on!"

"Nah, I want to know what you doing over here in my apartment complex. You know I run this shit over here."

"No, you run while taking the dick from everybody over here! How you manage to fuck every nigga out here? That shit sick."

"Bitch, I ain't fucking nobody but yo' nigga!"

"See, that's where you wrong because I don't have a nigga. Therefore, you ain't fucking nobody but ya trifling ass baby daddy." Before I knew it, the girl was running up on me like she was about to do something. Too bad she ran dead into my fist. I had swung hard as hell too, causing her to fall out on the ground.

"Bitch, I will be getting a restraining order on you!" she yelled. I could already see her eye turning black.

"Run up, get knocked the fuck out, bitch! I'm not ya average big mouthed ass female. I lay hoes out! Better ask some damn body, even though I'm sure you already knew that. So I don't even know why you just tried it like that and bitch, you can't get no restraining order on me! I live here!"

"Watch me!"

"Nah, bruh, you watch me!" I yelled and kicked her ass in the mouth. After that, I didn't even stay to chit chat with her anymore. I went and got straight in my car and pulled off.

Two hours later, I pulled up to the warehouse and parked around the back. The vibe was off to me and I felt like I was being watched. Everything in me told me to just leave and not look back. I had never gotten this feeling before when I was here. I continued to get out of the car though, and walked up to the back door and knocked.

"What's up?"

"Bring them birds out!"

"They gone fly or…"

"Open this damn door, Echo! I ain't got time to play tonight," I said, interrupting him. Something already didn't feel right and he wanted to play. He opened the door smiling at me.

"The boys about to head out now. Gone head and open up the secret compartments."

"Okay, but Echo, can we do this fast? Something don't feel right," I said, tapping my foot.

"Girl, chill, ain't nothing gone pop off out here," he said cockily, as the guys with the product started coming out. I walked to my car and opened up the secret compartments. Then I walked back over beside Echo and watched the other guys. I was still tapping my foot nervously. The longer it took the more anxious I became.

"Echo, please tell yo' boys to hurry up, dawg. I'm not playing when I say something don't feel right." My stomach was doing flips and my head had started pounding.

"Damn, ma. Please don't tell me you done started using the product. You bugging for real and that ain't a good look." I rolled my eyes at this ignorant motherfucker. I didn't expect him to understand good and bad vibes, but he could have at least respected my wishes about them hurrying up.

"Fuck this, I'm out! Whatever they ain't get to load, I'll be back for it some other time," I said and got ready to head to my car.

"FREEZE, POLICE!" I heard someone yell. Next thing I know, we were being surrounded by all kinds of cops. Blue and red lights were flashing along with flashlights. My mind ain't fool me! I knew I was getting a bad vibe. I should have just turned around as soon as I felt it, but it was way too late for any of that now. "GET DOWN ON THE GROUND, NOW! NOW!" I heard the cops yelling. I was in shock and I couldn't move. Before I knew it,

I felt a pair of hands shoving me down to the ground. After I was on the ground, I felt a knee being pressed into my back.

"Ouch, what the fuck you doing?" I yelled. I didn't get a response though. All I got was my face pushed down in the dirt on the ground.

"GET THE FUCK OFF OF HER, DAWG! THAT'S A FUCKING FEMALE! THE FUCK WRONG WITH Y'ALL. SHE DON'T GOT SHIT TO DO WITH THIS!" I heard Echo yelling.

POW! POW! POW! POW!

I heard the gunshots ring out, but I couldn't register what had happened until I saw Echo's bloody body fall to the ground next to me.

"Oh my God, y'all shot him! Why the fuck did y'all shoot him? Why did y'all shoot him?!" I yelled out, but closed my mouth when I felt a nightstick hit me in the back of the head hard as hell. I was no longer able to focus. I was slipping in and out of consciousness as I felt the nightstick strike me in the head repeatedly. *What the fuck was going on?!*

***

"Ms. Banks… Ms. Banks… Ms. Banks!"

I heard someone yelling my name loudly. My eyes flew open and I took in my surroundings. I was in a fucking holding cell at the jail. That's when everything started to hit me at once. I remembered everything that had happened and now I was pissed! I cocked my head to the side and gave the officer that was calling my name a nasty look.

"What the fuck do you want?"

"Ma'am, there's no need for all of that. I just came to get you and let you know that you are free to go. When the police pulled up last night, they said that you were standing off to the side talking to a male. All the guys that we questioned said that you were just a friend that they had called over to chill. They stated that you were unaware of what was going on. Of course, we didn't believe them at all being that the car they were loading drugs into was yours. But, the chief insisted that we let you go. All he asked for in return is that if you are questioned by the news or anybody about the killing of Emanuel Fields, you stay silent. He needs for you to act like you don't remember a thing. A favor for a favor," the cop explained, making me want to slap the shit out of his ass as he let me out of the holding cell. They had killed Echo for no fucking reason and now they wanted me to remain silent about it.

"Fuck y'all pigs! Give me my shit so I can fucking go!" I yelled. The officer walked off and I followed behind him. He went to the back and I stood at the front waiting for him to bring me my things. He returned within minutes with a bag that had my cellphone and purse in it.

"Here you go. Your car was towed… I don't know where to though," he said and smirked at me. I snatched my shit from him and headed for the door, but I stopped mid-stride when I heard him call out to me. I turned around and waited for him to say something. "I'd lose the attitude and humble myself if I was you. You may be walking out of here today, but there are still a lot of officers that want your fucking head. Therefore, watch your back, kiddo," he said and winked.

"You watch your fucking back!" I yelled back and then got the fuck out of there before he tried to lock me up again for threatening him.

Once I got outside on the sidewalk, I pulled my cellphone out and powered it on. I was so thankful that it was still charged up. I looked at the time and it read 10 in the morning. I had definitely had one hell of a Friday night. There's no way anyone could have had a worst Friday than me.

I dialed Hazel's number and prayed she answered the damn phone. I know we had just started hanging out and all, but I really fucking needed somebody right now. This was the perfect time to see if she was as solid as I thought she was. It would also help me figure out if she was worth me trying to build a friendship with. Yes, I was open to giving everyone a chance, but you at least had to be solid and down to ride for me.

"Bitch, what happened to you last night?" Hazel asked as soon as she answered the phone.

"Girl, I will explain later. Right now I need a huge favor."

"Anything."

"Listen first and then you can answer the question."

"Nah, I mean it. We girls now and I'm the type of friend to be there for my friend if they need something. Bitches love hollering about having a bestie, woe, right-hand, left-hand, my bitch, or my sister. But the question is will you be there for your *bestie, woe, right-hand, left-hand, bitch* or *sister* when they need you? That's what these females don't understand. It's more to it than just labeling a bitch as your right-hand or whatever. Half of these bitches won't even ride for their home girl, for real. Too much fake shit be going on for me to even think about befriending a bitch if I don't feel like they solid. Yeah, the lil' names and shit be cute. Having somebody to hang out with be cool. Having somebody to talk to be nice. But I look at it like this, if you get too close to a snake it's gon' bite your ass, and it don't matter if you know the snake is there or not. A snake is a snake…" Hazel carried on before I finally cut her off. What she was saying was some real ass shit, but now wasn't the time!

"I know that shit's right. But check this out, Hazel. I got locked up last night and I need for you to come get me."

"Girl, I'm sliding on my shoes and heading for the door now," she said before yelling for her boyfriend to watch their daughter.

"Okay, but you should know that it's two hours away."

"I'm on my way. Send me the address."

"Bitch, bet!" I said and hung up the phone. I was thankful as hell for Hazel.

Two hours later. Hazel was pulling up in her red 2002 Honda Civic. I quickly hopped in the passenger seat. I had just been sitting in the same spot not doing shit. I was on my phone for a while until the motherfucker went dead. Then to top it off, I was hungry as hell. I could have walked down the street and got something to eat, but I didn't want to move out of my spot just in case Hazel showed up earlier than she was supposed to.

Twenty minutes had passed by and Hazel hadn't said anything. I appreciated the silence at first because I needed to clear my head. I guess Hazel knew that and that's why she remained silent. After another 20 minutes had passed by, she finally opened her mouth to talk.

"You good over there?"

"Yes, I'm straight. Some bullshit just transpired last night. I don't really want to go into detail about it right now, but I know it was AK's fault."

"Bitch, say no more! We 'bout to pull up on that ass right

now!" she yelled and sped up. I laughed a little bit because she was definitely with the shits.

We finally made it back into town and was pulling up at my old apartment complex. We hopped out the car and headed straight to Akeem's apartment. I covered the peephole as Hazel banged on the door. A couple of seconds passed by before we heard somebody moving around. We heard the locks being unlocked before the door came open.

"Ay, what the fuck happened last night? I been getting calls all fucking morning. I couldn't even hit your line because I didn't know if you had got locked up or what," Akeem said and lowered his gun as soon as he saw it was me at the door.

"YOU SET ME THE FUCK UP!!!" I screamed before charging at him.

"What the fuck you talking about, Mony?!" AK asked while holding on to my arms so I couldn't hit him.

"Shit got real last night! Echo is dead and I was locked the fuck up! I only got out because Echo's people had my back. Oh, and the chief wants me to pretend like I didn't witness Echo getting murdered for no fucking reason! You wanted me to go so bad last night! Why, Akeem? Huh? I know it was you that set me up!" I yelled, trying to break loose so I could introduce my hands to his stupid ass face!

"Wait, what? Hell fucking no! Watch out, ma," he said and pushed me to the side. He went straight across the hall and started banging on the door. "Nadia! Nadia, get the fuck out here!" It didn't take long before she came to the door with a silk robe on that was wide open. It revealed her matching bra and panty set.

"Yes, daddy?" she answered and smirked. But that smirk left her face fast when she saw me. "What is she doing... here?"

"Shut the fuck up! Why you set Harmony up when I told you to leave the shit alone?" AK asked her.

"You didn't say that," she said casually.

"FUCK ALL OF THIS TALKING!" Hazel screamed before she hauled off and popped Nadia in the mouth with her fist.

"Y'all bitches gone stop putting y'all hands on me!" Nadia yelled.

"Fuck you!" I yelled back.

"Would y'all chill?!" AK asked looking back at me and Hazel.

"No, forget both of you! I see y'all still fucking around and shit and apparently plotting on a bitch! Don't worry about it though. I got something for y'all," I said and laughed a little bit. *These motherfuckers gone make me kill them!* "Let's be out," I said looking at Hazel.

"You sure? I'm still in a fuck-a-bitch-up mood and I hate for it to go to waste," Hazel said as she stared Akeem and Nadia down.

"Big bitch gone, damn," AK said.

"I got yo' big bitch, nigga!" Hazel yelled before I pulled her on down the hall. If I wasn't so pissed off about the bullshit that was going on, I would have been laughing. Hazel was a trip!

The first thing I did when I got home was take a shower. Then I grabbed a bottle of gin and went and got in the bed. I rolled me up a couple of blunts and started my turn up session. After the night I had, I needed to relax. There was still so much shit going on in my head that I just didn't want to think about. It may have been early, but that didn't stop me from drinking and smoking myself to sleep.

CHAPTER 4

NADIA

I was beyond shocked to see Harmony standing outside of my door this morning. I don't know what the fuck had gone wrong, but she was supposed to be locked up. Then she had the nerve to have that ugly ass bitch, Hazel with her. Hazel had been dying to be her damn friend for years now. I guess Harmony couldn't wait to replace me.

Then there was stupid ass Akeem. I thought he was banging on my door because he wanted some. But no, he wanted to check me about some bullshit. I don't know what it's gone take for him to act right when it comes to me. He needs to understand that Harmony is done with his ass. I'm the bitch that wants to be with him. Fuck Harmony and fuck Carrie too. He was my nigga now. I don't care what he says.

After Harmony and her little sidekick left, I tried to get AK to come inside, but he didn't. Instead, he went back across the hall and slammed his door. I tried calling him, but he didn't answer. I guess he calls himself ignoring me now. I'll give him some time to himself.

I was currently in my room getting dressed. I had some important business to take care of now that I knew Harmony was out. After I finished getting dressed, I pulled my hair back into a ponytail and slid on my shoes. I grabbed up my purse and keys and headed out the door. Hopefully this business didn't take long because I had to go to work. I needed all the money I could get now since Harmony had moved out. Yeah, AK was going to take care of my rent, but I had other needs. Once I get him where I want him in this relationship, I won't have to work at all.

CHAPTER 5

CASANOVA

Yesterday was a long and boring Saturday for me. Charles and Elle were both plain. Charles didn't do anything but go to work. Then when he came home, he sat in the same spot for hours, looking over papers. My sister wasn't any better than him. She woke up extremely early just to clean the house. After she was done cleaning, she showered and studied for the rest of the day. In between all of that, her and Charles managed to say a few words to each other.

I didn't really mind too much. I mean, I was bored... very bored, but my plan had worked. I was staying under the same roof as Charles and that's the only thing that mattered to me. Sean had been blowing my phone up since late Friday night. I guess he expected me to be at the house when he returned that night. I hadn't talked to him yet, and I didn't plan to no time soon. My main focus was Charles. I was feeling him and I wanted him for more than his money.

He didn't know that though. Yes, he was crazy about me and we had even gotten a little close when Elle was away from home. But this whole arrangement between us was strictly about sex. He made that clear from the jump. He just wanted and needed sex.

That was cool at first, but I wasn't going for it now. I wanted sex, money, and him. I planned to get all of those things, too. It was easy moving in here. I mean, with Elle being so caring and all. She couldn't wait to help me with whatever I needed.

Now that, that was done, all I had to do was get Charles to fall head over heels for me. It wasn't going to be easy though. Charles hadn't said a damn thing to me since I'd been here. I planned on changing that though.

I didn't bother Charles Friday or Saturday night. I wanted to make sure Elle didn't usually come down in the middle of the night. Since she hadn't come back down here for two nights straight, I figured she wouldn't be coming down any other nights. I didn't expect for things to be so easy when it came to fucking around with Charles while staying in his home, but he was sleeping right across the hall from me. Everything seemed to be in my favor and I was going to take advantage of it.

It was Sunday and we all had retired to our rooms for the night. I had been lying in my bed for the last couple of hours, doing nothing. I had decided to wait and see if Elle would come down one last time. Since she still hadn't made her way down here I figured the coast was clear. I slid out of my bed and stripped out of all of my clothes. Then, I crept out of my room and eased my way inside of Charles's room.

I couldn't see much because the room was so dark, but I could hear him snoring lightly. I lifted the cover up at the bottom of the bed and crawled up to his waist. He didn't have on anything but a pair of briefs. I started stoking his dick softly through his underwear. He moved a little bit, but he didn't wake up. That was my cue to go ahead and pull his dick out.

Once I had his dick out, I took the whole thing into my mouth. It tasted so good and smelled even better. I slowly started bobbing my head up and down. Suddenly, his snoring stopped and the covers were being yanked back. I looked up at him, even though I couldn't really make out his face in the darkness.

"What the fuck?" he mumbled.

"Relax, it's just me," I whispered.

"Well, I know that. Elle wouldn't dare do no shit like this. Speaking of Elle, what are you doing? She could easily catch us right now."

"Would that be so bad?"

"What do you mean, Nova?"

"Enough with the questions," I said before I started back sucking his dick. I just wanted him to hush and enjoy this. I didn't care about Noelle. She didn't deserve Charles and she didn't know what to do with all of this man. I did. I heard Charles let out a small moan and I smiled to myself. I stopped what I was doing and climbed up on top of him. I sat right on his hard dick and started to move my hips. *Fuck a condom, I want and need to have this man's baby!*

I don't know what it was about Charles, but he changed my outlook on a lot of shit. Before, all I cared about was getting to the money. It was fuck love and get money, but that changed after the first night we had sex. Charles made me want more and I wanted more with him. Nobody else mattered to me. Only him.

My mom was going to be so disappointed in me, but I didn't care. The way Charles made my body feel was indescribable. I continued to ride him as I thought about a future with him. If Charles hadn't fucked me like he loved me that first night, we wouldn't be in this position. I was fine with us just having sex, but he changed that. It was his fault I wanted more.

Charles and I made love for hours before we finally stopped to take a break. After we both caught our breaths, we started right back up. I had orgasms back to back, but that didn't slow down our lovemaking session. Charles's stamina was out of this world and I was determined to keep up. I don't know if the possibility of getting caught turned him on and kept him going or not. Or if he simply just missed me that much that he refused to stop.

Our lovemaking sessions had slowed down these days, so he could have just missed me. Either way, I didn't care. We continued to have sex until we both were satisfied and fell asleep.

***

"Charles! Charles! You're going to be late for work!" I heard Elle scream out. It sounded like she was coming down the steps.

"Shit! what are you still doing in here, Nova?" Charles hissed as he quickly sat up in the bed. I rolled over on my side to face him.

"I must have fallen asleep," I said yawning. It was true I had fallen asleep, but I had woken up hours ago. Instead of getting up and going back to my own room, I snuggled up close to Charles and went back to sleep. Now we were waking up in the bed together as Elle made her way to his room.

"Get up! Why you just lying there?"

"Okay, but I can't go back to my room. She's coming."

"Just get up and hide! Damn, Nova." I rolled out of the bed naked and went into the large closet.

"Charles, you didn't hear me calling you?" Elle asked as she came storming into the room. I had just slid the closet door shut when she came barging in.

"What time is it?" I heard Charles ask in his sleepy voice.

"It's well after seven o'clock. I guess I'm about to head to school after I check on my sister."

"Why are you just now coming down here and you're going to wake her up?"

"Because I thought you was already gone and yeah, why?"

"Elle, let her sleep. She's probably tired."

"Yeah, I guess you're right. I'll just see her when I get home then."

"Elle?"

"What, Charles?" I heard Elle ask sounding slightly bothered.

"I love you."

"Yeah, love you too," she mumbled before I heard her shut the door. I waited for a few seconds before I came out of the closet.

"Do you have to go?" I asked, pouting.

"Yes," he said as he slid out of the bed and headed towards the bathroom in his room.

"Well, okay. I guess I will see you later on," I said before making my way back to my room. The sex I had with Charles last night had been the best between us thus far.

I grabbed my robe out of my room and went to take a shower. After I finished showering, I went back to my room and sat on my bed naked. I started putting lotion all over my body. When I was almost done, there was a knock on the door. After the knock, the door cracked open.

"I'm about to go, Nova," Charles said as he eyed my naked body. His eyes were full of lust. I stood up and slowly walked over to him.

"Have a good day," I said and pecked his lips. I strutted over to my bag that was in the corner of the room and bent down. I grabbed a pair of underwear and slid them on. Charles watched me for a few seconds more before he finally pulled himself away from my room door. After he left, I walked over to his room and started looking around. I quickly found one of his t-shirts and slid it on.

I climbed on the bed and started taking pictures of myself. I looked so good in his shirt, on his bed. I stopped snapping pictures and just laid back in the bed. I could still smell his scent and it smelled lovely. I closed my eyes and started rubbing all over my body as I thought about Charles. I was really feeling him and the sex we had. I felt like I wanted to love him.

He may have been my sister's boyfriend, but that was starting to become irrelevant. Not that it ever mattered. I really could picture myself having this man's baby. I know I only wanted him for his money before, but like I said, I wanted more from him now. I laid there and fantasized about him more. Just when I had slid my hand inside of my underwear, my phone started ringing. I jumped at the sudden noise, and quickly sat up to answer the phone without looking to see who was calling.

"Hello," I said slightly agitated.

"Hey, Nova."

"London," I said as I rolled my eyes. If I had known it was her, I wouldn't have answered.

"Listen, I've been wanting to talk to you, but I decided to give you some time."

"What is it, Lon?"

"I didn't tell Harmony."

"Okay, and?"

"And I realized my loyalty belongs to you and not your sisters. Look, can we meet up and talk? Where are you at?"

"I guess," I said. I didn't want to meet up with her, but she hadn't told anybody my little secret yet, so maybe we could still be friends. It all depended on how things went. I was still pissed with her, but I would hear her immature ass out.

"Great!"

"Meet me at my condo in an hour," I said and hung up the phone. I needed to go check on shit, especially after the way Rio had acted the other night. I had to make sure he hadn't messed up anything when it came to my condo. If I wasn't so set on getting Charles for myself, I would have gone and stayed over there.

I'm sure Charles would have picked up the payments for it. I'm going to have to ask him about it, but either way I'm still going to stay here. That way I can see him daily and keep up with his relationship with my sister. I want and need Elle out of the picture.

She needs to just let him go or I'm going to have to get very fucking manipulative. I know she isn't going to let him go though, especially after she pretty much told me that they were working on their relationship. But, not if I can help it!

I went back to my room and got dressed. After I was finished, I straightened my weave out until it was bone straight. Then I grabbed my purse and headed out after sliding on a pair of heels I had brought with me. When I pulled up to my condo, I saw London. I hopped out of the car and she met me on the sidewalk.

"Thanks for meeting up with me."

"Yeah, no problem."

When we got up the stairs to my place, I let us in and walked around. Everything seemed to be in order. That was a good thing. Now, all I had to do was go up to the front and make sure shit was still straight for now. I would do that when we left out. I walked over to the couch and took a seat beside London.

"I don't have all day," I said tapping my foot. She had just been staring at her phone for the last five minutes.

"Sorry… I was thinking."

"About what? You made it seem like you knew what you wanted to say over the phone. I met up with you, now talk."

"I freaked out the other day, Nova. The first thing that came to my mind is if you would cross your own sister you would cross me."

"Bitch, no one is worried about you or your broke ass boyfriend. Trust me. I'm trying to make a living out here."

"That's the thing. What if he wasn't broke? What if he had money, Nova?"

"Sweetie, listen at yourself. What if this… what if that. We both know Quez isn't about to get off of his ass to go out and make some real money. We both know you're not about to leave him and you're going to continue to support his broke ass. Those are the facts, my love. Therefore, you have no worries. You're my girl right?"

"Yes."

"Act like it and keep your fucking mouth shut about this Charles shit!"

"Nova."

"No, I'm serious, London. Mind your fucking business, or I'll tell Quez how you really make your money!"

"My lips are sealed. Look, I have to get going," she said before standing up and fixing her skin tight dress.

"Going to make money?"

"Something like that." I stood up and we both headed for the door. I locked up my condo and then we went back down to the parking lot.

"Well, I'm glad we talked," I let her know.

"Yeah, me too." I gave her air kisses before turning and walking away.

After I talked to the people in the office, I felt a lot better. They assured me Rio couldn't do anything because the condo was in my name. It didn't matter if he paid the bills or not. I already knew that, but Rio was crazy and I wasn't putting anything past him. I really just wanted to make sure that they wouldn't kick me out if he tried to bribe them or some shit. After I talked to them for a little bit, I came to the conclusion that they wouldn't.

I walked back to my car and got in. I felt a lot better knowing that London would be keeping her mouth closed. I couldn't believe she had, had the audacity to question me. She knows better than to think that I would go after Quez. Broke ass Quez out of all people. She was tripping with that one. I may be a lot of things, but a fool wasn't one of them and I would have to be a fool to ever settle for somebody or even go for somebody like Quez! *Broke niggas make me sick!*

CHAPTER 6

NOELLE

School went by fast this morning and I was thankful for that. I was able to attend both of my classes without running into Professor Black. I was going to skip class all together today, but it was close to exam time and I couldn't afford to miss any reviews we may have done in class. So I just decided to go on to class and I'm glad I did, being that both classes consisted of reviewing over things.

After my classes were over, I left campus right away and headed home. When I got home, I started studying some more. Charles still hadn't made it home yet, but he would probably be here soon. I had just finished up looking over one of my reviews when I heard Nova coming up the steps. I didn't even know she was here. Then again, I hadn't paid much attention.

"Hey, Elle. I didn't know you were home already."

"Yup, been here for about an hour now. How are things for you?" I asked and then looked at her. I had to do a double take because of what she had on. She had on a black pair of boy shorts with a red sports bra. Her hair was pulled up into a messy bun. Yes, she looked beautiful, but she wasn't at home.

"Things are good!"

"Are you sure? You were so upset the other day."

"I know what I was, Elle! That's the difference between me and most females. I get over shit quick and move the fuck on!" she snapped. I was just checking on her so I don't know why she felt the need to get so snappy. But, that was Nova for you.

"I'm home," I heard Charles say as he made his way inside of our home.

"Hey, how was work?" I asked. He didn't answer me right away. He just stood in the middle of the floor eyeing Nova.

"It was… umm… good. Yeah, it was good. Your dad and I have been getting a lot done lately," he said, still looking at Nova.

"That's good," I said back. The way he kept looking at Nova was really bothering me, but I decided not to say anything.

"Charles! I'm glad you're home," Nova said smiling brightly.

"Oh, why is that?" Charles asked as he looked at me now.

"I need help getting the rest of my things from my old home. I could use the muscle and I'm not ready to face Sean alone. The whole situation is still fresh on my mind," Nova said looking hurt.

"I thought you said you were over it?" I asked.

"Not now, Noelle! So Charles, what do you say?"

"Sure, I would love to help you. When do you want to go?"

"Now!" Nova said and took off down the steps.

"Charles, what is all of that about?" I asked.

"What are you talking about?"

"You know what I'm talking about!"

"No, I don't. I just got off of work and I'm tired. I'm not in the mood to argue with you. You're the one that wanted your sister to stay here, so don't start!"

"Don't start? You walked in here and you couldn't take your eyes off of her! You say you're tired, but you're all for going to help her."

"Well, I just won't help her then!"

"No, no, she needs help. You can go on. I guess I'm just overreacting. I just want us to get back to how we used to be, that's all," I said, calming myself down.

"We will, baby. But, we need to do something about this only having sex three times a year."

"Us only having sex three times a year doesn't have anything to do with our problems."

"Yes it does, Elle. If we had sex more, I never would have cheated on you!"

"Oh, so you're finally admitting to it?" I asked as a single tear slid down my face. Yes, I wanted him to admit to his wrongs. But hearing him finally say it didn't make me feel better like I thought it would.

"Baby, come here," he said softly as he made his way over to me.

"No," I said, full blown crying now. I stood up and tried to make my way to my room.

"Elle, please don't do this."

"You cheated on me, Charles?"

"Why are we discussing this again?"

"Just leave me alone," I said barely above a whisper as I went on to my room.

I climbed in my bed and cried some more. Why was this my life? Why was I still hurting from the mistake Charles had made? I shouldn't have felt this way. Especially after that night I had with the professor. My life was a mess. It didn't matter how hard I tried to fix it because nothing worked. Nothing made me feel better. Everything just made me feel worse… Except for *it*. The cocaine instantly crossed my mind. *Elle, don't do this,* I thought to myself.

CHAPTER 7

PROFESSOR BLACK

I walked into my office that I had at my home and took a seat behind my desk. I leaned back in my chair and looked around the room. Her face was everywhere in this room. On the walls in beautiful picture frames. On my desk in beautiful picture frames. Hell, she was even the screensaver on my laptop.

Only thing I hated is I only had one picture of her. One picture of the lovely Noelle Banks. I had no choice but to work with what I had though. I had gotten her picture off of the school's website. It was the picture that was on her school ID. I took that picture and made a thousand copies… literally.

I needed to see her beautiful face at all times. I had to see her beautiful face at all times. That's why her pictures were all over my office. I even have her picture on my phone too. I'm in love with her and she's in love with me, she just doesn't know it yet. I fell in love with Noelle the very first day I saw her. She was only a freshman in college then.

She was the first one to my class that day. She came in and sat right at the front. I didn't pay her much attention when she had first come in because I was busy preparing for my class. But when I looked up, I was amazed by her beauty.

See, Noelle has this natural beauty. This natural beauty that only seems to work for her. Her chocolate skin seems to glow at all times and God, that gets my dick so hard. Her beautiful bright eyes have this twinkle in them that never goes away. I get lost in those eyes every time I see her. Then there's her curly, thick, long, black hair that makes me want to just sniff it and then inhale deeply. But, what tops everything off is her angelic face. She has the face of an angel and there isn't anyone who can tell me different.

That girl has had my heart captivated for years now. I just never acted on it in the past. I know she's young, but age isn't anything but a number. My ex-wife was a little younger than me and that didn't stop anything. That's why I refuse to let it stop anything when it comes to Noelle.

I know she's scared when it comes to us, but she has to let that fear go. She has to let it go so she can follow her heart. She needs to just do exactly what it is that she wants to do, like she did that night when she came to dinner.

I knew cocaine was exactly what she needed to loosen her up. That's why I introduced her to it to start with. It worked like a charm too. She rode my dick so fucking well that night that I was tempted to kidnap her just to make sure she wasn't giving it to anybody else.

I know she has a boyfriend and all, but that's the least of my concerns. If he was doing his part as a man, I would have never even come close to having Noelle in my house. I knew after that night that he wasn't satisfying her the way that she deserved to be satisfied. He wasn't giving her the attention that she needed. But, that's okay, because a grown man like me stays ready to cherish something so beautiful.

That's why I regret letting her leave my office so easily. I should have continued to force her to stay. But, I simply wasn't in the mood anymore. I hadn't meant to flip out on her the way I did, but I just couldn't help it. She had made me so mad. She was trying to leave me like my ex-wife had done, and I just wasn't going for it.

I wish I could have seen Noelle's face today at school though. I got there super early and I left super late. I still didn't see her. I didn't run into her or anything. She had to be avoiding me. But that's okay, because she can't avoid me for much longer.

CHAPTER 8

HARMONY

I had pretty much slept my whole weekend away. Same thing goes for my day. It was Monday after four o'clock, and I was just now getting up. After that long ass Friday night, I was exhausted. I guess it's safe to say that I had caught up on my sleep. I may have been well rested, but there was still so much on my mind.

I sat up in my bed and looked around. It was so quiet and relaxing that I almost wanted to go back to sleep. Instead, I forced myself out of the bed and headed to the bathroom. I took a long hot shower that seemed to wake me right up. After my shower, I brushed my teeth and threw on some relaxing clothes. I didn't plan on leaving my house at all, especially after the shit that had gone down. I wasn't scared or anything. I was just cautious. Shit wasn't right around this motherfucker and I needed to start figuring things out immediately.

The whole thing with Echo was still fresh on my mind. He may have killed my nerves every time I went to get the product, but I wouldn't have wished death on him. He didn't deserve that shit at all. What killed me the most is he was only concerned about me. He died because he spoke up about the way that they were handling me.

I wish he wouldn't have said anything now. That probably

didn't matter much though. The police would have still found some dumb ass reason to off that man. I'm pretty sure of that. That's just how fucked up things were these days. To top it all off, them motherfuckers wanted me to lie. They wanted me to act like I hadn't seen a damn thing. Then, that one police officer had the nerve to tell me that there were still cops that wanted my head.

To be honest, I didn't give a fuck about any of that. Watch my back, my ass! I was dead ass serious when I told him that he had better watch his back. I didn't give a fuck about no damn police watching me. I had gone on my last drug trafficking trip that night and I didn't plan on doing it again. So they could watch me all they wanted to. Hell, it would help me out because I planned on watching their asses too. Therefore, they would be watching me, watching them, and I meant that shit.

For all I knew, they could have been plotting on taking me out next. Okay, maybe I was being a tad bit paranoid. But, you could never be too sure these days. I just wanted to be ready and alert. That way they wouldn't catch me slipping. All I know is they better watch their backs out here in the hood. Niggas don't fuck with cops around here so they would be lucky to make it around here for even a day.

Our city cops didn't even come out this way. The only way they were coming was if they got a phone call, and they barely showed up then. When and if they did, it would be late as hell.

Those out of town cops better ask some fucking body, before they pop up missing around this bitch. And that's nothing but the truth.

I went to my room to get my sack of weed and a pack of Cigarillos. When I got to my stash, I realized I didn't have anymore weed left and that pissed me the fuck off. I grabbed up my phone and sent a text to this nigga that lived right outside of town. He was a city boy. I only knew him because I used to mess around with him when Akeem and I used to be on one of our many breaks.

I hadn't talked to him in a while, but I hoped his number was still the same. Buying from one of AK's people was out of the question. I no longer trusted him in any kind of way, so I would not be buying shit from his people. I didn't know what the fuck him and Nadia were on now, but they were some snitch ass bitches in my eyes.

Me: What's up?

Kelly: Who dis?

Me: Harmony… is this Kelly?

Kelly: Wat up, ma?

Kelly: Ya dis Kelz.

Kelly: Long time no talk!

I stopped texting and laughed at him texting back to back.

Kelly used to want me bad. He was the one that stayed telling me that Akeem wasn't no solid nigga. He tried to make me his over and over again. He even begged me to stop going back to Akeem. But, I wasn't going for it back then. Boy, I sure do wish I would have listened. Then I wouldn't have had to go through none of this crazy shit.

Me: lol I know right! You busy?

Kelly: Lil bit. Why wats up?

Me: Ran out of green... wanted to get some from you.

Kelly: Bet that up! I can be on the way.

I smiled at the phone before letting him know my new address. That's what I used to like about Kelly. He would drop whatever he was doing just for me, unlike Akeem who would text or call back hours later. After he was finished with whatever he was doing, of course.

I got up and threw on some booty shorts with a crop tank top. I brushed my hair out and allowed it to hang. I hadn't seen Kelly in a while and I wanted to look nice for him or whatever. I was single now and I was going to start acting like it. After I was done getting cute, I went back to the living room and waited for Kelly. A good 40 minutes had passed by before I heard him knocking on the door. I got up to let him in.

"Damn, Harmony, you still finer than a motherfucker," Kelly said as soon as I opened the door. I smiled at him and moved to the side to let him in. The smell of his cologne instantly hit my nose. He smelled so fucking good and looked even better.

Kelly was mixed with black and white. His skin looked like it was kissed by the sun. It was so smooth and light. He had these bright green eyes that were to die for. He wore his hair really curly at the top; it was this sandy brown color, and it was shaped up around the edges. He had always been cute, but damn. He was sexy as fuck now.

I closed the door and walked over to the couch behind Kelly. We both took a seat and I just looked at him. He saw me looking at him and started laughing. I immediately looked the other way. Ain't no shame in my game, but I was pretty sure I had been gawking at this man.

"Don't try to look away now. I already saw you staring a nigga down and shit," he said. I looked over at him and he was smirking.

"Wasn't nobody staring at you, nigga," I said and rolled my eyes.

"Yeah, okay. Where yo' boy at?"

"Who?"

"Oh, so you an owl now?"

75

"Shut up!" I yelled and started laughing.

"You'd make a sexy ass owl though. No doubt."

"You so corny!"

"Little bit, but nah, for real. Where yo' boy at?"

"Nah, for real who?"

"Akeem, dumb ass girl."

"Don't be calling me dumb, Kelly!"

"Dumb ass, sensitive ass, girl," he said and smiled at me.

"Whatever! Ain't nobody sensitive."

"You avoiding my question like the fucking plague ain't you?"

"Okay, okay. We not together anymore."

"For how long this time, Harmony?"

"For good."

"Yeah fucking right. I been knowing yo' ass for years and that ain't never proved to be true."

"Well, it'll prove to be true this time. You see I moved."

"That don't mean shit. Bitches move all the time to get away from niggas. Then a few weeks later that same nigga be laid up in their new shit."

"Bitches?"

"You know what I mean. Damn. Told you, you were sensitive."

"I am not. I'm for real though. I'm done with him."

"You always say that."

"No, I don't. I usually say I'm so sick of his ass and all kind of shit, but I've never said I was done with him before and you know it."

"Okay, you right."

"Yep, turns out he was fucking my best damn friend. That's why I up and moved."

"That's fucked up! Told you to leave that fucking clown alone."

"Blah, blah. Where the weed at?"

"Damn you a chronic. Can't even sit and talk. You already asking for the weed," he said laughing, as he pulled out a Ziploc bag full of weed. "I brought this just for you. This that pressure right here, shawty. It ain't that weak, country ass, bullshit yo' little boyfriend be selling."

"I see you still be talking a lot of shit, nigga!" I said laughing, as I took the Ziploc bag out of his hands. I opened it up and smelled it. He was right when he said it was some pressure. I'm talking straight gas pack!

"Whatever, sensitive ass girl. Roll that dope up!"

"Who the chronic now?"

"Yo' ass still!" he yelled and I started laughing.

"How much my dude?"

"It's on me."

"Shit, say no more!" I grabbed a cigarillo and broke it down, then I placed some of the weed in my weed grinder and grinded it up.

"Look at you. Yo' sexy ass think you doing something, don't you?"

"Nigga, please," I said as I rolled up the blunt.

"Give me that shit," he said and snatched the blunt out of my hand when I was done rolling it. He placed it between his sexy ass lips and lit it up with a lighter he had pulled out of his pocket.

"Oh, you tripping now! You know the rules. If you roll it, you light it!"

"And if you got it for free you shut the fuck up!"

"Okay, okay, you got me. Do ya thing, playa." He hit the blunt a few times and passed it to me. I hit that shit harder than I should have and started choking. I immediately passed the blunt back to him.

"Rookie ass! Hit that damn blunt, girl," he said as he refused to take the blunt from me. "Told you this not that lil' bullshit you usually be smoking on." I rolled my eyes as I hit the blunt a few more times before passing it back to Kelly.

My ass was high already. While Kelly was hitting the blunt, my phone dinged. I looked down and noticed I had a text from Akeem. I looked over at Kelly to see if he was paying attention to me. He was looking right at me.

"Ain't nobody paying you no mind! Gon' 'head and text ya lil' dude back." I couldn't help but laugh.

"Shut up! You must be since you know that's who texted me. All in my shit and shit, and that ain't my dude!"

"Sure." I smiled at him before opening up the text from AK. As I was opening up the text, a few more started to come in.

Akeem: Carrie texted me and told me you living over that way now.

Akeem: She say some dude in yo shit.

Akeem: Who the fuck you got over there Mony?

Akeem: ???

Me: Don't fucking worry about it!

Me: And tell ya bitch to mind her fucking business!

Akeem: Don't make me come over there!

"That nigga tripping ain't he?" Kelly asked, scaring me.

"Damn, you nosey as fuck!"

"Lil' bit."

"No, a lot," I said as my phone dinged again.

Akeem: I'm on my way! That nigga better be gone when I get there!

"He a funny lil' motherfucker ain't he?"

"He a stupid little motherfucker," I said as I snatched the blunt out of his hand.

"What he about to come over here and do?"

"Knock at the damn door because he sure as hell not about to get in here."

"He better hope that's all he does. I'd hate to have to put that thing on yo' lil' boyfriend tonight," Kelly said smiling, as he pulled his gun out and placed it on the table. "I ain't with no bullshit. I lay niggas out, ask questions never."

"Sounds like me."

"Girl, stop!" Before I could respond, there was a loud knock at my door.

"Open this fucking door up, Mony!" I heard AK yell. It hadn't even been three minutes. That told me right away that he must have already been over here. Carrie hadn't told him shit. He probably seen my car outside and saw Kelly come up here. Now he was tripping.

"Nigga, take yo' clown ass on!" Kelly yelled towards the door. I started laughing hard as hell. I was already high as fuck so that shit was super funny. I passed the last bit of the blunt back to Kelly.

"Open this damn door and say it to my face, nigga!"

"Nigga, fuck you! Get the hell on!" Kelly yelled back. Ten minutes had passed by and AK's crazy ass was still at my door banging. Kelly and I were ignoring the fuck out of him and talking like he wasn't at the door. Kelly was rolling up another blunt to smoke on. I was still extremely high, but I wasn't about to tap out on the blunt. After he was done rolling it up, I stood up.

"Come on, let's go back to my room." Kelly didn't say anything back. He just stood up and grabbed his gun and the weed off of the table. He passed me the blunt and I headed on back to my room.

Once I was in my room, I grabbed my lighter off of the

nightstand and lit it up. Kelly placed his gun and the sack of weed on the nightstand. Then he stripped out of his clothes. Under the clothes he took off, he had on a white t-shirt and a pair of basketball shorts. I'll never understand why niggas wear so many damn layers of clothes.

He sat on my bed and slid in the middle of it, and placed his back on my headboard. I guess I didn't have to tell his ass to get comfortable. I smoked on the blunt some more before passing it to Kelly. His eyes were low as hell. I swear he looked even sexier when he was high.

"Take this shit off," he said as he pulled at my booty shorts. I stood up and slid them right off. My black thong and fat ass was on full display. "Damn, come here." I climbed on top of him and straddled him. He hit the blunt and then blew me a shotgun. He tried to blow me another one, but I snatched the blunt from him.

"I need the real thing."

"Chronic."

"You gone stop calling me that shit," I said laughing before hitting the blunt.

A few more minutes passed by before the knocking at the door finally stopped. I guess Akeem had finally gotten tired. I was glad too. I had other shit on my mind for the night and he was low-key throwing me off with all of that damn knocking. We hit the blunt a few more times before putting it out.

"So where your girl at, Kelz?"

"Oh, now you wanna ask about a girl? While you on top of me with ya fat ass poking out just right," he said licking his lips.

"Shut up! I know you ain't got no girl."

"That's right, because if I did, I wouldn't even be here. All that cheating shit played the fuck out. You can't be a real nigga if you lying and cheating on ya girl. Real niggas keep it real with everything, no matter what it is."

"And finally somebody said it!" I yelled, giggling. I swear I was feeling lovely.

"Girl, get yo' high ass off of me," Kelly said laughing, as he shoved me to the side and got off of the bed.

"Where you going?"

"To find something to damn eat. A nigga got the munchies."

"Look at you!"

"Look at me," he said smirking as he made his way out of my room. I sat up in my bed and smiled. This was going to be a fun evening and night too... hopefully. I checked my phone and saw I had a couple of texts from Hazel. She wanted to know what I was up to. I shot her a quick text back and told her I would call her later and if I didn't, I would get up with her tomorrow.

CHAPTER 9

CASANOVA

I stood at the top of the steps listening to my sister carry on with Charles. She was pissed about the way he was looking at me. On the other hand, I loved it. One thing I've learned about Charles is he can't help but to appreciate a nice body. It doesn't matter what he is supposed to be doing.

After I heard Charles slip up and admit that he had cheated, I smiled to myself. Elle got all upset and I could hear her storming away. That girl is so pathetic and weak. It sounded like Charles was about to go after her, so I quickly made my way on into the living room in just a sports bra and some yoga pants.

"You ready?" I asked.

"Umm, almost. Just let me go downstairs and change right quick."

"Take your time."

While I waited on Charles to go and get ready, I walked to the kitchen and poured myself a tall glass of wine. It was so good and defined. After I finished my glass up, I peeped down the steps to see if Charles was coming. When I realized he wasn't, I tiptoed around the condo until I found Elle's room.

She was in her bed crying. She was balled up while holding

tightly onto a pillow. The only light that was on in the room was the lamp that sat on the nightstand beside her bed. I could see her face. She looked so troubled and pained as the tears rolled down her face. I almost wanted to comfort her. *Almost.* I tossed my hair over my shoulder and made my way back to the living room.

"How is she?" Charles asked as soon as I stepped back into the living room. I jumped a little bit because he had slightly scared me.

"Oh, she's fine. Let's go," I said and then led the way out of the house once I had grabbed my purse. "Who's car we taking?"

"We can take mine."

The ride to my house was a quiet one. Charles was quiet as hell and I didn't like that one bit. The whole entire ride, he looked like he was deep in thought. I bet he was thinking about Noelle. I could just sense it.

That's understandable, but what he needed to realize was the damage was already done. All he could try to do now was fix it. He had admitted his wrongs. Now he needed to make Noelle accept that so that they could move on. Or they just needed to break up, which was what I was hoping for.

Breaking up was the answer because Elle was insecure as hell. There's no way she would ever let the shit go. Knowing her, she would self-destruct at the thought of it alone. She didn't like conflict because she couldn't take the pressure. That's why she had chosen to do the right thing all of her life.

What she failed to realize is that she was grown now. This was the real world. The flowers, rainbows, and fucking butterflies were gone. That fairytale ass life was gone. It was time for her to find herself and stop being weak. If she didn't, this cold ass world was going to ruin her. It was going to chew her up and spit her right back out. I was going to have to talk some strength into that girl. Only because I needed for her to be strong and leave Charles though.

When we pulled up to my old house, I noticed Sean's car in the driveway right away. I figured he would be here. We hopped out of the car and made our way to the door. I was going to knock, but I decided against it and just let us in with my key instead. When we got inside, we saw Sean laid out on the couch with a bottle of brown liquor in his hand.

"Nova, you came back," he said and sat up on the couch.

"No, I came to get my shit," I said before heading up the stairs.

When I got into my old room, I pulled out my suitcases and started to pack up all of my things. I could hear Sean downstairs talking to Charles. He was begging him to help him get me back. Charles said something about giving me space and then he let him know that I was staying with him and Noelle. Sean sounded grateful to hear that. I quickly finished up packing my clothes that

I missed the most then headed back downstairs.

"It's good to hear she's with y'all, man. That mean she plans on coming home eventually," I heard Sean say as I walked into the living room. Him and Charles were both sipping on a beer.

"Let's get something straight. I'm staying with them because I choose to. Not because I need to and not because I plan on coming home to you."

"Baby, can we please just talk?" Sean asked. I swear everybody wanted to talk today.

"Charles, go upstairs and get my shit. It's the first room to the left. Just walk down the hall and you will find it," I said.

"I'm on it," Charles said and hopped straight up, putting his beer down. I guess Sean and I were making him uncomfortable because he was more than ready to excuse himself.

"Talk," I said. I really didn't care to hear what he had to say though.

"Casanova, why are you doing this?"

"Doing what, Sean?!"

"This! First YOU cheat on ME. Then, YOU have the nerve to leave ME. This shit ain't right! What kind of breed of bitch are you?!" he yelled and slammed his hand down on the table. He was upset! I smiled and then chuckled a little before responding to him.

"No, what kind of breed of bitch are you? I'm not the one in here looking pathetic right now… you are!"

"You know what? Get the fuck out! I don't even know why I'm trying with you. I should have known you was cheating from the jump. You were always so anxious to take them out of town trips. Out of town trips that your friends didn't go on. How could you possibly go on a trip that many times by yourself just for the hell of it? I don't know how I missed it to be honest. Give a bitch money, love a bitch, and still get hurt by that bitch! What level of fucked up is this?" he asked while walking back and forth. He looked like he was about to flip out.

I wish I could say I cared, but I didn't. It was always about the money with Sean. I wanted money and he gave it to me. He spent check after check on me. There was no limit when it came to money with him. I was in love with his money not him. Had Charles not fucked my head up with his sex, I would still be here. I wasn't after just money anymore. I was after a man, and I was going to get him by any means necessary.

"The way I look at it, I did you a favor," I said, as I saw Charles make his way downstairs with the bags. He headed straight outside to take my things out.

"A favor? You cheating and leaving me counts as a favor now?"

"Count your blessings, Sean," I said before sashaying out of his home.

When I got outside, Charles was already inside of his car and waiting for me. I got in and let out a long sigh. I felt like Sean really was lucky. I mean, he should be thanking Charles if you ask me. If it wasn't for him, I would still be with him and putting a major dent in his pocket. I never would have loved him. Therefore, he was lucky I moved on.

"Why was you so hard on him?" Charles suddenly asked.

"Because I don't want or care about him."

"How can you say that?" he asked and then gave me a funny look. The way he looked at me pissed me off. He knew I had two guys from the jump, but now he wanted to play like he cared about Sean's feelings, knowing he didn't give a fuck about Sean. If he did, he would have never fucked me. He had only seen and talked to Sean a couple of times anyway, so he could stop the act.

"The same way you can say that you love Elle, while fucking her sister. You don't love her, Charles."

"I do love her. I just needed sex. You were willing to give it to me so I went for it."

"I wasn't willing to do shit! Last time I checked, you came at me first. You wanted me first. So get your facts straight!"

"Nova, calm down."

"No, I'm not going to calm down! You in this car looking down your nose at me like you're some kind of saint. Like you not tearing this pussy up every chance you get! Like you not fucking me raw and nutting all in me! Negro, please don't play with me!"

"Nova, we not gon' be able to keep fucking around if you gon' act like that."

"Cut it out. I've been playing your game, but let's be real for a minute."

"What you mean by that?"

"I mean you act like you not feeling me like that when I know you are. Tell me you don't want me in more ways than one, Charles."

"Nova, I... I don't... I mean."

"No need to explain the facts."

"But, the facts are I'm with your sister. I'm happy with her. She's all I need."

"She's all you need? Are you sure about that?" I asked as I reached over and started rubbing on his dick through his pants. A small moan escaped his lips and I knew that I had him. "That's what I thought," I said before undoing his pants. I pulled his dick out and started giving him head as he drove. If I had to suck his soul out for him to act right, I would. This man was going to be mine.

"Shit, Nova. You gone have to stop! I can't drive like this!"

"Fuck that!" I sat up and yelled. "Go to the nearest hotel!" I leaned back over and took him in my mouth once again. I felt him step on the gas and speed up. *It was game time and I didn't plan on striking out.*

CHAPTER 10

NOELLE

I heard the door slam shut and that told me that Nova and Charles had left. I saw Nova standing at my door not too long ago, but I was too upset to say anything to her. I got out the bed and walked into the living room. I peeked out the window by the door and saw them both getting in Charles's car. I slowly walked back to my room and got the cocaine out.

Tears were slowly rolling down my face as I made a couple of lines on my nightstand. I did it just like I had saw the professor do. Once I thought the lines were perfect enough, I just sat there for a minute. I was going back and forth with myself. I had never felt this way in my life. For the first time in my life I felt like I had inner demons and I was going to have to battle them one way… or another.

I quickly leaned down and sniffed up the first line. My face immediately went numb like it had done that night at the professor's house. I smiled to myself and laid back on the bed. I wanted to do the other line, but I couldn't move after the first line. Twenty minutes had passed by before I finally was able to sit up and do the next line.

I wanted to feel exactly like I had felt that night with the professor, but it just wasn't the same. I felt pretty good, but not as good as I had felt that first night. I decided to just put the cocaine back up after I realized I wouldn't get as high as I did before. I felt like I needed something, but I couldn't figure out what. I just sat in the same place not doing anything.

A couple of hours had passed by and Charles and Nova had yet to return. I was losing my mind just sitting here. I got up and grabbed my phone before making my way into the living room. I called Charles a couple of times, but he didn't answer. I called Nova once and she didn't answer either.

After sitting on the couch for a few more minutes, I decided to call Harmony. I needed somebody to talk to. I needed someone to be here for me, but I didn't have anybody. Harmony hadn't answered the phone either and I really needed for her to. I got up and headed to my bathroom. I got in the shower and allowed the water to fall down over my head.

I just stood there for 10 minutes straight, thinking to myself. Then I washed up and quickly got out. I put on a pair of sweatpants with a Nike t-shirt and headed for the kitchen. I scanned through our liquor bar before I decided on some Patrón. I knew I didn't need to be drinking, but I was driving myself insane.

After I had poured myself a glass of the Patrón, I went back to the living room and sat down. I sipped on the strong alcohol a couple of times before throwing caution out the window and chugging the entire glass down. It was a short glass, but I instantly felt the liquor start to take over.

I got up from the couch and went to put my flip flops on. After I had them on, I grabbed my phone and my keys and headed out of the door. I jumped in my car and made my way out of the driveway. I drove around for a little bit with nowhere to go. It was better than staying home and drowning in my feelings though. I sped up the car and continued to drive around. The faster I went, the harder I was laughing.

I felt free and I was having the time of my life. I turned up the music and sung along to the Maxwell song. His voice was so beautiful. Before I knew it, I was pulling up in front of a house. I just sat in my car and stared at the house. I wanted to get out, but I didn't. I figured I would just continue to sit and stare. The alcohol had me feeling sluggish and I really just wanted to take a nap. I closed my eyes for just a minute.

CHAPTER 11

CARRIE

"I can't believe this bitch, man!" AK busted through my front door and yelled. I rolled my eyes up in my head at this nigga. We had just started back fucking with each other this morning and he was already fucking up.

He was the one that called me this morning, apologizing and shit. I knew his ass would be back. This shit wasn't new. I don't care how many times or how bad we got into it, we would always be back to fucking with each other. I mean, I'm his baby mama. I'm not going no fucking where! That's what these raggedy bitches needed to realize. Baby mamas rule the fucking world and we will always have the last say so when it comes to our baby's fathers. Females be falling for what these niggas be telling them and niggas will lie quick. The first words they love to scream is "I don't fuck with my baby mama." Lies, lies, and lies.

"Don't be coming in here with that shit!" I yelled at Akeem.

"Girl, what you talking about, and why you ain't let me know Harmony stayed over here? I get out my car to come see you and guess whose shit is parked out front? Then, I see that Kelz nigga glide his ass up the fucking steps. I knew he was going to fuck with her because his ass ain't never been over here before!"

"My nigga, I really don't give a fuck about shit you talking about right now," I let his ass know before lighting up my cigarette.

"I was up there knocking on that damn door for forever! Then, the nigga gon' have the nerve to yell out and tell me to get on, like I'm some lame nigga! Harmony is my bitch! I should have shot that door the fuck down!" he continued on. I put my cigarette out in the ashtray, then I lit up the blunt I had rolled earlier instead because this nigga was tripping!

"Mama, we hungry!" Lil' Cam came in the living room and yelled.

"Boy, if you don't get your ass out of here! Don't you see me doing grown-up shit! Don't you barge your little ass in here no more! I told you to stay in that damn room and watch your sisters and brother!"

"I was watching them, Mama! We got hungry and then the game just froze! What we supposed to do now?"

"GET YO' LITTLE ASS THE FUCK OUT OF HERE, CAMERON! THAT'S WHAT THE FUCK YOU CAN DO! DAMN, YOU SEE ME TRYING TO ENJOY MY FUCKING BLUNT!" I yelled pissed. I swear my kids were gon' be the death of me.

"Yeah, get the fuck out, lil' nigga," Akeem added. I turned around to face him so quick because I didn't know who the fuck he thought he was talking to.

"Akeem, don't you say shit to my child! If you want to say something to one of my kids, you better go in that room back there and get your daughter! But what you not gon' do is say shit to my other kids!"

"You ain't my daddy, nigga," Lil' Cam said while mean mugging the fuck out of AK.

"I bet I'll whoop yo' lil ass like I am!" AK yelled and then started laughing. But Lil' Cam didn't find shit funny because he charged at him and started swinging on him.

"Cam! Cam!" I yelled at him, but he just kept on swinging on Akeem. Akeem was laughing hard as hell by now.

"Ari, you better get this lil' nigga before I knock his ugly ass out in here!" Akeem said between laughing, but I knew his crazy ass was serious so I finally got up and grabbed Lil' Cam after I set my blunt in the ashtray.

"Take yo' ass back in that room, boy!" I yelled and pushed him towards the back.

"Fuck you, Mama! I wanna go stay with my daddy!" the little nigga had the balls to yell. Before I could respond, the other kids all came running from the back.

"We hungry!" they all yelled at once.

"What you just said?" I looked at Lil' Cam and asked. I ignored the other kids completely because I wanted this little motherfucker to say that shit again.

"You heard me! I said I want to go stay with my daddy!" he yelled again.

"Chez, go get my black leather belt!" I looked at my other son and said.

"Why, Mama?" he asked looking scared.

"Go get that fucking belt out of my room before I beat your ass too!" He took off out the living room and down the small hall. He came back in the living room out of breath and passed me the belt.

"This shit wild," AK said laughing.

"Shut the fuck up, Akeem. Cameron, get your ass back there on that bed!"

"Mama, no, I'm sorry," Cam said as he started crying.

"You wasn't crying when you was talking to me like you grown!" I yelled at him. I snatched his little ass up by the arm and pulled him to the room he shared with his brother. "Get on that bed!" He fell out on the floor and continued to cry while pleading for me not to whoop him. "Don't make me tell you again because if I do, it's gone be worse!" He quickly got up off of the floor and laid across his bed. "Don't even try that shit. Strip!"

"But, Mama, you said for me to get on the bed."

"Take them fucking clothes off! Yo' little ass is about to learn tonight!" He continued to lay on the bed like he hadn't heard me. I walked over to the bed and snatched his ass up and started going across his head with my belt. This little nigga had me fucked up!

"Ouch! Ahhh! Noooo!" he cried out like he was getting killed.

"Didn't... I tell... yo' ass... to take them fucking clothes off! Don't you... ever... in yo'... black ass life... cuss at... a woman!" I screamed with each lick I was giving him.

"I'm sorry, Mama!"

"You... ain't... sorry... yet!"

"Ahhhh... ahhhh... yes I am, Mama!" he cried out. I finally stopped because my arm was hurting like hell.

"Now, take yo' ass to fucking sleep! You going to bed hungry tonight and you can forget about living with your daddy! He don't want your bad ass staying with him and his precious bitch! If he did, you would be with him, and you can tell him I said that shit too! Stupid ass lil' boy!" I turned off his light and walked out his room. I could hear him sniffling and shit once I got out in the hall. So I slammed his door shut and went back to the living room.

"Where is Cam, Mommy?" my daughter Cynthia asked. She was still standing in the middle of the floor with her brother Chez.

Chloe was in Akeem's lap playing.

"He gone to bed."

"Bed? Mama, it's too early for that," Chez said.

"It ain't too early for shit because that's where y'all going after y'all eat."

"But we haven't had our baths yet," he said.

"I know what y'all ain't had! Y'all can take a bath in the morning before I take y'all to your grandma's house. Now, take your sisters back there to their room and y'all stay in there. I'll come get you when the food ready."

"Okay, Mama," he said. He walked over and picked up Chloe off of AK's lap. Then he grabbed Cynthia's hand and headed out the living room.

I walked back over to the couch and sat down. I got my blunt out the ashtray and lit it back up. Damn kids had done wore me the fuck out. I swear kids don't listen. You tell their ass to do one thing and they do another.

"You ain't have to whoop that lil' nigga like that. Should have let me knock his ass out in here. That nigga ran up on me like he was a grown ass man!"

"Shut the fuck up. I'm 'bout sick of your ass, AK."

"Stop blowing up my fucking phone all of the time then."

"Last time I checked, you was blowing up my phone this morning! Don't be catching an attitude with me. It ain't my fault Harmony upstairs getting her back blown out like the hoe she is!"

"Bitch, you the hoe!"

"Nigga, get out and tell your bitch the next time I see her, we banging! Stupid ass called herself jumping on me the other night."

"Girl, stop. Ain't nobody jumped on yo' big ass! But I'm out," he said and headed for the door. I didn't even try to stop him because I wanted him gone. He hadn't done nothing but pissed me off the whole entire time he was here.

I was serious about banging with Harmony on sight though. Stupid bitch had left my face swollen and hurting for days! Who the fuck kicks somebody in the damn face?! Stupid ass bitch had to catch these hands. She was lucky I didn't go up to her shit and beat her ass there.

After I finished my blunt, I got up and went in the kitchen. I opened the cabinet to see what I could feed the kids. I decided on some Ramen Noodles for their asses. I opened the packs up and cooked it on the stove all at once. After it was done, I fixed their plates and set them on the table, before going to get them so they could eat. Their bad asses came flying out the room like they hadn't eaten all day. While they were eating, I decided to drink on some Kinky. The bed would definitely be seeing me after I put these kids to bed.

CHAPTER 12

HARMONY

I woke up wrapped up in Kelly's arms. He was still knocked the fuck out and snoring like hell. I don't know why he was sleeping so good. It's not like he had gotten any last night. It wasn't my fault either. He was the one that decided he wasn't going to give me any dick. I don't know why he was playing because we had, had sex in the past.

"Nigga, get your ass up!" I yelled and threw his arm off of me.

"What the hell?" he sat up in the bed and asked. Then he looked back at me and smirked. "Don't be waking me up because you mad you ain't get no dick. Sensitive ass girl!"

"Shut up! You wrong for that shit," I said and rolled my eyes. I couldn't help but to smile at his sexy ass though.

"Don't trip, ma. Just play ya cards right and then I'll dick you down real proper like," he said and licked his juicy ass pink lips.

"You play too fucking much, man!"

"Lil' bit. But what time is it?"

"It's six in the morning," I said after checking my phone. I noticed that I had a missed call from Elle. I would just have to call her back later.

"Six in the who? Girl, you tripping for real. I'm going back to damn sleep."

"No you not either!"

"Watch me!" he yelled. He laid back in the bed and pulled the covers up over his head. A few seconds hadn't passed by good and his ass had sat back up quick as hell.

"What?"

"Roll us a blunt right fast, baby. You know… wake and bake shit in this bitch." I laughed at his stupid ass before climbing out of bed to roll us up a blunt.

"Know I'm down!"

"Hell yeah, I know your chronic ass down."

We smoked a couple of blunts in bed before Kelly went right back to sleep. I couldn't go back to sleep though because I was wide awake. I got up and took a shower before going to the kitchen to cook breakfast. This nigga already had me tripping because I cooked for no one but my damn self! I guess it's a first time for everything though.

CHAPTER 13

CASANOVA

"Hurry up, Nova," Charles hissed at me as we made our way inside of his and Noelle's home at five in the morning.

"I'm right behind you!" I yelled.

"Be quiet."

"For what? I don't know if you noticed or not, but Elle isn't here."

"It's five in the morning. What you mean she's not here?"

"Like I said, she isn't here."

"How do you know?" he asked as he headed down the hall towards her room. "You're right. She isn't here," he came back into the living room and said.

"No shit! Her car wasn't even in its parking spot." Charles ran over to the window and peeked out. "Where the hell is she?"

"I don't know. She might be out creeping like you was doing." Charles ignored my comment and checked his phone.

"Fuck! She called me a million times. I didn't even hear my phone ringing last night."

"That's because I turned it on silent when we got to the hotel."

"Why would you do that, Nova?"

"Charles, do not start with me. Plus, you weren't even worried about your phone last night."

"That's because I figured it would ring if anybody was trying to reach me. I can't believe we lost track of time again."

"I didn't lose track of anything."

"Whatever. I'm going to get in the shower before I head to work."

"Okay," I said and then watched him walk off.

I fucked Charles so good last night that I had him screaming out he loved me. That shit sounded like music to my ears. I'm not going to lie though, he had me screaming out all kind of shit too. He called himself pulling out of me last night because we weren't using a condom, but I wasn't going for it.

He begged me to slow down, but that only made me speed up. Then when he was about to nut, he tried to lift me up off of him. Nope! Didn't happen, because I locked down on his ass and sped up even more. It's safe to say he nutted all in me. I didn't hop off of him after he had done it either. I remained on top of him and refused to let him pull out. We fell asleep that way.

I headed down the stairs and went to my room. I didn't stay in there for long though. I wandered out of my room and went into

Charles's room. I could still hear the shower running so I stripped out of my clothes. I walked into the bathroom and slid in the shower behind him. It was so steamy that he hadn't even noticed I was there. I kissed his back and he turned around fast as hell.

"Nova, what you doing?!"

"Relax, baby."

"No! I'm not going to relax. What if Noelle comes?"

"Who cares?" I asked as I started rubbing up and down his chest.

"I care!"

"I think we established last night that you don't care. Now, take me!" I yelled and jumped on him. He held me up in the air. His arms were wrapped tightly around my thighs. I leaned in and kissed him. It wasn't long before I felt him slide his tongue in my mouth. I started sucking on it right away. The more I sucked on his tongue the wetter I got.

"Damn, Nova," Charles said after he had pulled away from our tongue sucking session.

"I know, baby," I whispered in his ear seductively. He lowered me down a little bit and plunged right into me. I moaned loudly as I allowed him to take me to my climax.

By the time we both had an orgasm, I was exhausted. The only thing I wanted to do was take a nap, but I could do that after I finished washing Charles up. We washed each other at the same time, then we rinsed off and got out. Charles gave me a towel before heading back into his room.

I quickly dried off and then went back into his room also. I picked my clothes up off of the floor and made my way back to my room. I allowed the towel to drop to the floor before I went and climbed into my bed. I snuggled up under my covers and started to drift off to sleep right away. I heard my door open up and my eyes popped open.

"I'm heading out," Charles said standing over me. I sat up in the bed and reached for him. He leaned down and I pulled his face closer to mine. I kissed him deeply and then let him go.

"Alright, see you later." He leaned down and pecked me on my lips before exiting my room.

Small shit like that is what told me that Charles wanted me like I wanted him. He was just afraid to hurt Elle. He tried to play like this thing between us was all about sex, but that was a lie. If it was about sex, we would straight up fuck and go our separate ways. That wasn't the case with us. We made love to each other and we cared about each other. If he didn't care about me, he wouldn't come to tell me bye in the morning before he left. You could tell a lot about somebody by simply reading in between the lines. After I was done thinking about Charles, I closed my eyes and went straight to sleep. All of that sex had me exhausted!

CHAPTER 14

PROFESSOR BLACK

I woke up early this morning like usual to get ready for school. I slid out of my bed and went to take a hot shower. After I finished my shower, I got dressed and headed to the kitchen. I started the coffee maker up and then went to the fridge. I pulled out a pack of bacon to cook because that's what I had a taste for. When the bacon was done, I toasted me a couple of pieces of bread. By the time I was done cooking, my coffee was ready and the pot was full.

I fixed me up a cup and drank it as fast I could so that I could head out. When I walked outside, I saw an unfamiliar car parked in my driveway. I slowly walked over to the car and looked in. It was Noelle. Her head was tilted back and her mouth was slightly opened. She looked exhausted. I reached down and grabbed the handle of her door. To my surprise, it was unlocked.

I leaned in and the smell of alcohol instantly hit my nose. I scooped her up in my arms and closed her car door with my foot. Then I headed inside of my home after I had struggled to unlock the door. I went straight to my bedroom and laid her down on my bed. She looked so fucking beautiful.

After I had just stood there staring at her for 20 minutes, I leaned down and kissed her soft lips. They were so soft and they made me want to kiss all of her. I took all of her clothes off piece by piece and then I stuck them in my closet. I needed to save her clothes for later because I had plans to sleep with them since her scent was all over them.

I walked back over to my bed and sat down. I continued to look at her some more before I climbed on top of her. I started kissing all on her. My lips touched every single part of her body. The more I kissed her, the hornier I got. So instead of stopping when I thought she was waking up, I continued to place my lips all over her chocolate body.

CHAPTER 15

NOELLE

I woke up and it felt like someone was on top of me. I wanted to open my eyes, but my head was pounding. I felt kisses being placed all over me and that made me open my eyes right away. I looked down and he was on me, kissing my… naked body. What was going on here.

"What are you doing?!" I asked, yelling.

"Pleasing you," he said and then continued to kiss on me.

"Stop! Get off of me."

"Get off of you, Noelle? I'm just giving you what you want."

"How do you figure I want this?"

"Because I found you asleep in your car this morning. Outside of my house. All you had to do was knock last night. I would have let you in."

"Professor Black, that is crazy!"

"Is it?"

"It is."

"Tell me… what were you doing out there?"

"I… I… I don't really know."

"Well, I do. You finally came to your senses and realized that I'm what you need. I'm glad you did too, because I didn't like the way things were going between us. I would have hated to have to flunk you, but I would have done it."

"I don't understand. Please get off of me."

"You say that like I'm trying to rape you."

"I say that like I'm uncomfortable with the situation."

"Noelle, you never cease to amaze me. You know you really should look into acting."

"Acting?"

"Yes, acting. All you do is act. But, you can stop the act now. That good girl image was destroyed that night you gave me a piece of you."

"I didn't give you a piece of me! I made a mistake! I was vulnerable and you took advantage of me."

"Does telling yourself that help you sleep at night?" he asked, as he continued to lay on me and look me in my face.

"I don't know what you're talking about."

"STOP THE FUCKING ACT, NOELLE! I'M SICK OF IT! YOU KNOW DAMN WELL WHAT I'M TALKING ABOUT!"

he yelled while shaking me. "My God," he mumbled and rolled off of me. I quickly hopped out of the bed after him.

"Where are my clothes?" I asked as I looked all around the room. The water works had begun and I couldn't see clearly because I couldn't stop crying.

"I don't know," he said mocking me.

"Please help me find them! I need to go."

"I don't understand you. You come to my house on your own and then you wake up and act like I forced you here."

"I told you I don't know what happened last night!"

"That's bullshit. You got drunk... started missing me... and came over. You must have been too drunk to get out of the car last night. That's what happened."

"I wasn't drunk last night!"

"Yes, you were, and you smelled like alcohol when I got you out of your car." That's when it hit me. I had gotten drunk last night and I did drive here. I had nowhere else to go so I came here. I don't know why, but I did. I closed my eyes for a second and I don't remember anything after that. I must have fallen asleep. I have to do better! This is all getting out of control.

"Can you just give me my clothes?"

"I told you I don't know where they are. Your keys are over here on the dresser though," he said as he started to get dressed. I looked at the clock on the nightstand and saw that it was seven in the morning. I walked over to the nightstand and snatched my keys before marching right out of his room.

"See you at school!" I heard him yell out. I ignored him and checked a few of the hall closets. It didn't take long for me to find the coat closet. I snatched one at random and put it on. I zipped it all the way up and left out of his house immediately. I was glad that I was small because his coat swallowed me whole.

I got in my car, started it up and sped off. I didn't think about my phone until I was halfway home. I looked around and luckily, it was in my passenger seat. I proceeded to my house, deep in my thoughts. I prayed Charles was gone because there would be no explaining this. Although I would have loved to hear about what happened last night, being that I checked my phone and he hadn't even bothered to call me.

I unlocked the door to my condo and went straight to my room. I was so happy when I pulled up and didn't see Charles's car anywhere. I took the coat off and shoved it in the bottom of my clothes basket. Then I hopped in the shower to get rid of the smell of Professor Black. When I got out, I threw on anything and pulled my hair up into a bun.

I picked up my book bag and just stopped. I set it back down on the floor and decided I would not be going to school. I needed this day off. No, I didn't have the professor's class, but I couldn't even fathom the thought of running into him. So instead, I headed to the kitchen to make myself some tea. That would calm down my nerves.

After I was done sipping on my tea, I went downstairs to check on Nova. I had seen her car when I pulled up so I knew she was here. I cracked her door open and looked in. She was fast asleep. She didn't budge or anything. I closed her door back and went back up the stairs.

I had been watching cartoons all morning and now it was going on noon. That didn't motivate me to get up and get my day started though. I just continued to lie on the couch and do nothing. I didn't have too many days of not doing anything, so I was truly enjoying it. Although, I should have had my butt in school. My mind was just too far gone for that.

"Good afternoon," I said to Nova as she neatly sat down in the chair across from me. She was dressed like she was about to have a photoshoot for the cover of a magazine. Her wavy bundles were pinned up on top of her head. Only a couple of strands of hair hung down in the front. She looked beautiful.

"Hi, how are you?" she asked, beaming.

"I'm fine."

"That's great, Elle. I thought you would have been pissed or upset about Charles not coming home until this morning."

"He didn't come until when?" I asked getting upset. Since I had left last night I didn't know he hadn't come home until this morning.

"After we got my stuff yesterday, he told me that he needed for me to get a hotel because he had stuff to do. He told me that he would pick me up after he finished. Next thing I know it was going on five in the morning and he was just now coming to get me. He asked me not to say anything to you, but what kind of sister would that make me?"

"I can't believe this."

"I couldn't either. I would have called and told you yesterday right away, but I didn't want to upset you. So I decided to wait and tell you."

"That's fine, Nova. Thanks for letting me know."

"No problem. But where were you this morning?"

"Huh?"

"Where were you? When we got home this morning you weren't here," she said and looked at me as if she was accusing me of something.

"I went to school," I lied. I hated to lie, but I couldn't tell her where I really was.

"That early? School isn't even open that early."

"How would you know, Nova?" She looked at me and smirked.

"I wouldn't. All I'm saying is if you were out creeping I wouldn't blame you."

"I was not out creeping."

"Well you should have been! Noelle, you are too fucking weak! You need to get some backbone, seriously! This world is going to fucking ruin you! You don't let your problems control you and break you down. You control and break your problems down!" she screamed at me.

"I don't know what to say."

"Don't say shit! Let it sink in. At the end of the day, I don't think this relationship is worth holding on to. Now, that's coming from your big sister. Think about it." She stood up and disappeared out of the living room.

Maybe Nova was right. I was too weak. I needed to find myself and take control. I made up my mind to talk to Charles as soon as he got home. Enough was enough. He was going to give me some answers about what he really wanted when it came to us. I would base my decision of staying or leaving on that.

***

I had studied, cleaned, and cooked dinner by the time Charles got home. Nova had left hours ago to do whatever. He came home looking tired as ever, but I refused to be considerate today. Usually, I would push what was on my mind to the back of my head and allow him to relax. That wasn't going to happen today.

If I was going to stop being weak, I needed to start right here and right now with Charles. After he changed his clothes and things, he came walking back into the living room where I was seated. He stared at me looking slightly pissed. I tapped the spot beside me and he came and sat down.

"Where were you this morning?" he asked right away.

"School. I got up and went to school after I noticed my boyfriend wasn't going to come home. I waited for you and I called y'all," I said calmly, but I was ready to test out being strong and standing up for myself for once. I may have been lying, but I realized he didn't deserve to know that. He didn't deserve to know a thing until he started being honest with me first.

"Noelle, I'm sorry. I had a lot to do yesterday and umm…" he said and then paused.

"You can save the lies, Charles! Nova already told me everything!"

"Nova did what?!"

"That's right, she told me. She also told me that you wanted her to keep it a secret."

"Baby, listen, about that."

"I'm not finished talking! She told me all about how you dropped her off at a hotel room and left her there all night. She says you didn't come back until this morning. So tell me what did you have to do that was so important yesterday? Huh?" I asked. His face relaxed a little bit and that made me angry. I couldn't understand why he would feel relaxed after I had told him how busted he was.

"Business, I was out handling business."

"All night long?"

"Yes."

"You listen to me, Charles, and you listen good. I refuse to keep doing this with you if you can't be honest. I refuse to continue to be lied to. So you can either come clean or you can get the hell out!"

"I'm not going anywhere! I pay the bills here! But you want the truth and I'm going to give it to you. Yes, I cheated. Do I regret it? Yes. Can I take it back? No. Can we fix us? I think we can. Just give me a chance, baby. I've never done anything like this before so I deserve a chance. I just got sexually frustrated. I had a couple of weak moments. But, I'm not willing to give up on us," he pleaded.

I know he was trying to be honest like I wanted him to, but my heart ached. I couldn't respond to him. I found myself going to my room and climbing in my bed just to cry into my pillow once again. I was proud of myself for being strong, but unfortunately it hadn't lasted.

I was really crying my eyes out when my phone started ringing. I didn't want to answer it, but I figured I could use the distraction. I didn't recognize the number, but I answered the phone anyway. At first the line was quiet. But, after a few seconds of silence, the person on the other end finally spoke up.

"I missed you today. I thought I would at least be able to see your pretty face in the hallways after you left my place so quickly."

"You stole my clothes!" I hissed into the phone. He chuckled a little bit before responding to me.

"I didn't. I told you I didn't know where they were."

"That's crap and you know it! I was fully clothed in my car!"

"You don't know that, Noelle."

"Yes, I do, Professor Black."

"Nope, you were knocked out when I spotted you outside of

my house. So, how do you figure you had on clothes? Either way, it doesn't matter. I've seen your naked body more than once now."

"I don't care to talk about this anymore! Look, can you just give me the grade I deserve in your class, please?"

"What's in it for me, Ms. Banks?"

I hung up on him. I didn't want to hear anything else he may have had to say. I already had a lot going on with Charles at the moment and he wasn't doing anything but making things worse for me. Maybe I was just going to have to fail his class after all. This man wasn't even playing fair. How was I ever supposed to keep up with him and this horrible situation I was in?

CHAPTER 16

HARMONY

Breakfast with Kelly had gone well. He joked and clowned around the whole entire time. He asked me 10 times straight did I poison his food because he didn't give me the dick. He was so damn stupid, but I liked him. I liked him a lot. It had to be a lot because I had cooked for this man. He tore that food up too. We smoked together one last time after we ate and he headed on out.

Now, I was sitting on my bed, bored, and looking crazy. I thought about smoking again since he had given me a Ziploc bag full of weed, but I decided I was good off of that for now. I picked up my phone and scrolled through Facebook for a little while, until a text message popped up on my screen. I clicked the message so that I could read it.

Hazel: Hey boo!

As soon as I read the message from Hazel, I remembered I was supposed to call her. I exited out of the messages and called her right away. It rung for a while and then it went to voicemail. I pulled the message screen back up because I was about to text her and cuss her ass out. I can't stand when folks have the phone right in their hands, but don't answer! I knew she had it in her hand because she had just texted me.

"Hello? You were about to get cussed the fuck out," I said into the phone as soon as I answered. She had called right back.

"My bad, but what's up chick?" she asked.

"I was just calling. I meant to call last night, but honey, I had got into some shit."

"Say word?"

"Word, but get up and let's go to the mall. You can bring your baby."

"It's cool. Her daddy will watch her. You know she a big daddy's girl. She not gone do nothing but cry the whole time we out."

"Girl, that's not good," I said laughing.

"I know, but I'm serious. But, I'll be over there when I finish getting ready."

"Okay, girl."

I hung up the phone and went to search for me something to wear. After I was dressed and ready to go, I went and sat in the living room to wait for Hazel. Twenty more minutes had passed by before I heard her tapping at the door. I grabbed my car keys and headed out the door.

"So, what you need to get from the mall?" Hazel asked once we were in my car and headed towards the mall.

"Nothing, I really just wanted to get out of the house."

"I feel you on that, girl."

We pulled up to the mall and headed inside. We went into a couple of stores and I bought a couple of things, but after a while, I was bored and ready to go. We went to the food court in the mall and I got us something to eat before we headed back to the car.

When we got back to the apartments, we headed to my place. I rolled us up a fat ass blunt and we smoked on it before we ate our food. It was the middle of the day by now and it really wasn't much to do. I swear I was bored as hell and I was missing Kelly already.

"I know what I forgot to tell you, Hazel."

"What's that?"

"Sexy ass Kelly was over here last night."

"City boy Kelly?"

"Girl, yes."

"Bitch, stop that lying!" she yelled, laughing.

"He was!"

"That's why yo' ass ain't hit my line last night then. You were too busy being fast over here with Kelly."

"I was not. We just chilled and I cooked breakfast for him."

"Oh, so you like him?"

"Duh, he wouldn't have been over here if I wasn't cool with him."

"I'm not talking about like that! I mean you really like that boy. Like you want to be with him."

"How you figure all of that, Hazel? You reaching now," I told her, laughing.

"I'm not reaching. Ain't no woman about to up and cook breakfast for a nigga if she ain't feeling him."

"Okay, you got me. I'm feeling him, but so what? We've been knowing each other for a while now and you know Akeem's ass is history."

"Girl, you don't have to explain. I'm not knocking you at all. Kelly is fine as hell. Always have been. I just knew you was feeling him after you said you cooked for him."

"Yeah, yeah. But, let me tell you about AK's stupid ass."

"What he done did now?"

"Girl, he got to texting me yesterday while Kelly was over here."

"Unt uh, what did his clown ass want, honey?"

"He knew Kelly was here. A few minutes after he had texted

me, he was at my door banging all loud and shit. He was already being nosey when he had texted me."

"That motherfucker is pathetic! Like fall the fuck back, damn."

"Girl, that's what I was saying."

"Straight up! Fuck that nigga. If he mad, he can stay mad. Better go fuck Nadia's nasty ass."

"That's probably all he's been doing!"

"Right, bitch!" Hazel yelled and we both burst out to laughing.

"I'm not about to play with you, Hazel!"

"I'm about to go anyway, heffa. I gotta get back to my baby."

"She ain't worried about you, she with her daddy!"

"Shut up. But I'll talk to you later."

"Alright, bye," I said as I let her out of my apartment. I locked the door and went back to lay on the couch. Ten minutes hadn't passed by good when I saw Kelly's name pop up on my phone.

"Hello?"

"Damn, you answered fast as fuck."

"I did not," I said smiling into the phone.

"You miss me yet?"

"Nope!"

"I ain't know you was a liar, Harmony."

"Whatever, what you doing?"

"Shit, lil' bit of this, lil' bit of that. You know how I move."

"I don't know a damn thing," I said and rolled my eyes. I was about to say something else when I heard a knock at my door. "Hold on, somebody at my damn door. I don't know who it is. 'Cause ain't nobody said shit to me about coming over here. You know what? Never mind. Motherfuckers gone learn to call before they pop up at somebody shit!"

"I did call. Now open this damn door up." I hung up the phone and walked over to the door. When I opened it, Kelly was standing there smiling at me.

"I don't know what you smiling for!"

"Because ya ass 'bout crazy with ya thick self," he said and squeezed my ass when he walked into my apartment.

"I'm not crazy. I was just chilling and didn't feel like being bothered."

"No, you were talking to me and didn't want to be distracted from that," he said and smirked.

"You swear you know something. What you doing back over

here?"

"I came to see you."

"Aww, that's sweet."

"Lil' bit."

"Hush, what you wanna do? 'Cause I wasn't doing shit in here."

"Turn a movie on or something." I went to Netflix on my TV and scanned through the movies until I came across *How High.* "Hell yeah, turn that shit on," Kelly said as he started rolling up a blunt. "We 'bout to be tripping in this bitch."

"And is," I said as I snuggled up beside Kelly on the couch. When he finished rolling up, we lit the blunt and started the movie. I was really enjoying the shit. AK and I hadn't just really chilled in forever. I missed simple shit like this. Kelly was steadily winning me over and I didn't mind at all.

"Oh, I know what I meant to tell you," Kelly said halfway through the movie.

"What?"

"I spotted some cops in the parking lot across the street. They in an unmarked car. Let me find out y'all hot with the police over here. Might have to cut your ass off. I don't fuck with no police," he said laughing, sounding like he was only halfway joking.

"Fuck them!"

"Look at yo' lil' gangsta ass. I like that, Harmony." I didn't respond, I just remained snuggled up to him. I guess them stupid ass police had finally found their way this way. But, like I said, they wasn't about to catch me slipping. They had started watching me so better believe I was about to start watching their asses right back!

CHAPTER 17

NADIA

It was late in the evening and I was lying in my bed, with AK between my legs, of course. His head laid on my stomach as he stroked my thigh lightly. He had finally come to his senses and started back fucking with me. Although he only ignored me for like a day, that day was long as hell though and I was miserable. I had missed his ass like fuck. All I know is he had better not been out fucking with no other bitches.

"Watch out," I said to AK as I tried to get up.

"What the fuck you doing?"

"I have to get in the shower. You know I have to work tonight. Plus, I got a stop to make so I have to get going."

"I thought you was off tonight?" he asked as I got off of the bed.

"Nope," I said and headed for the shower.

When I got out the shower and went back to my room, AK was gone. I swear he's childish as fuck. I know he calls himself being mad about me having to go to work, but I told him I had to go in tonight as soon as he came over. I didn't have time to worry about him though. I had shit to do before I went in to work.

I got dressed quickly and headed straight out of my apartment. I jumped in my car and sped down the street a couple of blocks. I parked beside this black car and got out. I tapped on the person's window and immediately heard the locks unlock. I opened the door and got in after I looked around to make sure no one had seen me.

"Good evening, Nadia."

"What's up?"

"Any news on Ms. Harmony Banks? I've been watching her all day, but she hasn't done shit, but go to the mall with some girl. Then some guy just went up to her apartment not too long ago. You know anything about him?"

"Wait a damn minute, officer. You asking too much, too fast. Slow the fuck down my G. I just got in the car."

"I'm sorry. I just want to take this bitch out so bad. I know she had something to do with what was going on that night. You called and told us yourself. Shit just went bad too fast."

"Look, y'all had the bitch. I'm not understanding why the fuck y'all let her out of jail!"

"We couldn't keep her. Everybody said she was innocent and just happened to be out there. Then, the chief bitched up after that boy got shot. He let her go thinking she would be some kind of help for us. But when the time comes, the last thing she is going to be is some help. She's going to be a fucking problem!"

"Y'all 'bout slow as hell. How you find out where Harmony stay at anyway?"

"I'm a cop, Nadia. Finding out shit is what I do."

"Yeah, okay, but ain't no telling who she fucking with now. So I probably don't know who the guy is."

"Well, I'm going to need for you to sit here with me tonight and wait for him to come out. We need to know who he is."

"Like hell you say! I gotta go to work," I said and opened my car door.

"Fine, I'll be in touch," he said as I got out the car. I quickly walked back to my car and hopped in. I sped off and headed to work. I hated I worked at a McDonald's that stayed open 24/7 because every now and then, I would have to work the night shift.

I got to work and clocked in right away. As soon as I put on my headset and went up to the cash register, I saw Carrie. Her ugly ass was working at the cash register right beside me. I rolled my eyes at her and prepared myself for my shift. A couple of customers came in and I took their orders. After they had their food, Carrie decided she wanted to fuck with me.

"So, tell me. What it's like to be a trifling ass bitch?" she asked.

"I don't know, but I'm pretty sure you can tell me a thing a two about what it's like."

"Bitch, fuck you. I can't tell you a damn thing about that. But, what I can tell you about is AK. He's been at my place a lot lately."

"I mean his daughter does live there."

"Trust me, he doesn't be coming to see her."

"Oh my God!" I yelled and walked to the back to find my manager. "Mark! I can't work with that thot ass bitch all night! I swear to God I can't!"

"Nadia, calm down and go back up to the front. Or you can just leave. It's up to you," he said and walked away.

"I hate this place, man. Bullshit ass job! I swear!" I went back up front and did my best to ignore Carrie. Going home was never an option, so this was about to be a long ass night. I could tell that already.

CHAPTER 18

CASANOVA

I had gone out for some drinks after I gave Elle that talk yesterday. The whole time while I was out, I couldn't help but wonder did my talk get to her. I needed that talk to get to her. I had given her the boost that I felt like she needed to be done with Charles, so hopefully she ended things with him. I feel terrible about lying on Charles, but I had to. Besides, all of it wasn't necessarily lies.

I sat up in my bed and looked around. Then I got up and slipped on my robe that I had spotted by the door. I walked outside of my room and headed up the stairs. I knew that nobody was home because it was well after nine. I went to the kitchen and grabbed a bottle of water. Anytime I would go out and drink, my throat would be extra dry the next morning.

After I finished up my water I went back downstairs to get my phone. It took a little while for me to find it since I was drunk last night and had dropped my phone somewhere. I finally found it under the bed. Then I went back up to the living room and turned the TV on, before taking my phone and making a call.

"Hey, Mommy," I said as soon as I heard her answer the phone.

"Is this my daughter?"

"Mom, stop."

"Nope, this can't be my daughter because I'm used to hearing from my daughter. I haven't heard a thing from you, stranger. So, who are you?"

"Mom, cut it out, damn! I don't know why you always have to start. You know if you don't hear from me I'm probably busy or something."

"That, or could be in a ditch somewhere dead."

"You are so dramatic! That's not even a possibility."

"I don't know that!"

"Well, who's fault is that exactly? You know what I called you to talk, but I'm not in the mood anymore."

"Honey, I'm sorry. I get nervous when I don't hear from you. You're the only one I can talk to and find out how you and your sisters are doing."

"Once again, that's your fault, mom! You know what?" I asked getting an idea.

"What is it?"

"You need to come home! You have been gone for years! You left and never came back. That's why no one wants anything to do with you."

"Nova, I don't know about that, sweetie."

"Well, I do! You're sitting there acting like you're so concerned about us. Well, come see about us and fix things with your other daughters."

"I just don't know how I would be able to pull it off. You know I watch the twins while their father is gone out traveling the world."

"Well, tell him to take a break and watch his daughters!" I yelled, getting annoyed. My mom's boyfriend had two twin daughters. My mother said they were three when she first started dating the guy.

"I can't ask him to stop doing what he loves. Traveling means everything to him. That's how he met me, you know."

"Yes, I know, and I don't care! Look, either you start planning your trip out here or I'm not going to continue to talk to you. It has been seven long years and you need to come make shit right!" I was being hard on my mom. I know that, but I had a plan up my sleeve and I needed her to bring her ass home for it to work.

"Alright, I'll see what I can do."

"Mom, just make it happen," I said and hung up the phone.

The plan I had was to get my mother here. Once I got her here, I could use her. I needed for her to come and be a big ass distraction. Elle is a sucker for love and sappy shit, so I know once my mom comes home and tries to fix things with her she's going to fall right into her arms. She will be so caught up with mom that she won't even be thinking about Charles. That's exactly what I needed, too.

I got up and turned the TV off in the living room before heading back down the stairs to my room. I went in my room and plopped down on my bed. After being out all day yesterday, I decided I would stay in today. I turned on some music on my phone and thought about how I was so close to making Charles only mine. I was deep into thought when my phone dinged and distracted me. I picked it up and looked at the message on the screen.

Rio: Sup stranger!

Hell no, my eyes had to be deceiving me, because I know this nigga hadn't texted me. I know he hadn't texted me after he fucked up my whole get money operation. There was no way in hell I was going to continue to fuck with him. I know what he thought, though. He thought since he had fucked shit up with Sean and I that I was available. He wanted me back and that wasn't about to happen.

***

I jumped up out of my sleep. I don't even know when I fell

asleep or how long I had been asleep, but I woke up out of the blue. I rubbed my eyes and checked my phone for the time. It was one in the morning. There's no way that I had slept that long. Charles or Elle didn't even think about coming to check on me. If they did, they didn't try to wake me up. Those inconsiderate bastards.

I got out of the bed and made my way right out of my room. It was dark so I couldn't see much, but I walked across the hall to Charles's room. I reached for the doorknob, but there was nothing there. That's when I realized his door was wide open. I walked inside and flipped the light on. His bed was empty. *Why the fuck was his bed empty?*

Rage instantly shot through my body. I headed out of Charles's room and headed for the steps. I took the steps two at a time. When I made it to the top of the steps, I went straight down the hall to Noelle's room. I was about to lightly open the door when I heard talking. I pressed my ear to the door so I could make out the words.

"Charles, why are you in here again tonight?" I heard Noelle ask. *Wait! Again?* I thought to myself. I was sloppy drunk last night so I didn't even bother going to Charles's room when I got back. I just went straight to bed. That was clearly a mistake on my behalf. If I had known that before, I wouldn't have wasted my day lying around. I would have been out trying to stir the fucking pot.

"I'm just trying to fix this shit between us. Isn't that what you

143

wanted? Ain't that why we had that talk yesterday? I gave you your truths." *Her truths? What the fuck did he tell her?*

"Yes, but you allowed me to lie in here and cry all day, Charles."

"I wanted to give you space, baby. I'm sorry. At least I did come in here before it was too late. Plus, I held you all night. You didn't like that?"

"I did. But, was you holding me because you wanted to? Or was you holding me because I couldn't stop crying?"

"I was holding you because I love you." *He what?* I was starting to get pissed even more after I heard Charles say he loved Elle. He had just told me the same thing a couple of nights ago, and to hear him telling her that made my blood boil.

"Really?" Elle's weak, gullible ass asked.

"Yes, baby. You wanted me to come clean and decide who I wanted and I want you, Elle. I'm not going to fuck up this time. You trust me?"

"Yes."

"Okay, then close your eyes and get some rest. You don't have anything to worry about anymore."

"You promise?"

"You know I do."

"I love you, Charles."

"I love you, Elle. So much." I backed away from the door. I just stood there staring at it. I kept telling myself not to bust in that fucking room and scream the truth. I made myself go back downstairs to my own room. I climbed in my bed, still pissed the fuck off. My mother had better get her ass out here and quick!

CHAPTER 19

NOELLE

My relationship with Charles is now better than ever. We finally talked and decided to try to patch up our relationship. Yes, he had cheated, but I decided to let that go. I mean I had done my dirt and Charles still didn't know anything about it. I planned to keep it that way too. There was no way I was coming clean about that to anyone. At least not right now anyway.

School ended a couple of weeks ago and it's no surprise that I failed Professor Black's class, although I know for a fact that I aced that final exam. The whole thing was pretty messed up. I knew I was going to fail though. The final week of class, he forced me to come to his office to talk to him. He wanted to discuss my options.

I was all for it at first. I went into his office ready to demand a passing grade. I had even come up with a couple of fake threats to threaten him with. But when I went into his office, I saw my clothes from the night I got drunk and went over there, laying on his desk. I lost it and I went off on him.

It's like I knew he had my clothes from the jump. But seeing them casually on his desk caused me to get upset. The smirk he had on his face when I saw my clothes hadn't helped either. Being strong when it came to Charles improved my relationship. So, I decided to take the same approach with Professor Black.

It's safe to say that was the wrong approach with the professor. After I went off on him, he went off on me right back. I went home and cried to myself that day because I knew what was in store. That still didn't stop me from going to take his exam. I gave that exam my all. I know for a fact I passed. But, the 45 on my exam said otherwise. Seeing that crushed my spirits at first because I was hoping for the professor to have a heart. I wanted him to do the right thing so bad, but he didn't.

I stayed upset for a couple of days after I saw my test results. Charles done his best to cheer me up and I appreciated that. I appreciated him trying period when it came to us. But, he didn't understand. He thought I was just crying because I had failed, but it was more to it than that.

After I cried until I wasn't able to cry no more, I decided to toughen back up. Being strong may have been the wrong move with the professor, but it was going to be the right move for my life. I decided I was done crying all of the time and instead of doing that, I was going to take action.

I went out to my school and signed up to retake the class online. While I was there, I filed a complaint against the professor. I didn't go into detail, but I did make him out to be a horrible teacher. Nothing was probably going to be done because it was just one complaint, but it was still worth doing. I was sure he would find out about it sooner or later. When he did, I hoped the news ruined his psychotic day.

Anyway, I originally wanted to retake the class on campus, but with a different teacher. That plan was shot down when I found out that Professor Black was the only professor they had to teach that class. So, I opted for the online class instead, although I felt like it was a lot more work than being in a classroom.

My online classes haven't started yet, so I'm just going to prepare myself for it, even though I don't have to prepare much. I already know everything there is to know, so I'm not worried about it that much. I'm just dreading all of the extra work I'm going to have to do.

In the meantime, I have been out job hunting. I'm not planning on leaving Charles anymore, but I still want to work. I've been craving to be independent lately. I don't know if it's because of my whole new attitude and outlook on life or what, but I want to do for myself. Charles understands, but Nova doesn't.

Speaking of Nova, something is up with her. I don't know what it is and I can't figure it out for nothing, but she has been the most bitter person lately. I tried to ask what was wrong, but she swore up and down she was fine. The way she looks at Charles and I when we show affection to each other, says different though. I told Charles I think she misses Sean, or maybe she just misses having someone period.

He doesn't seem to care too much about what's bothering her though. He even suggested that we kick her out if she continues to act like a bitch. I don't like that idea too much. She has nowhere to go. So what kind of person would I be to kick her out? Even if she is acting nasty towards us. I told Charles we should just give her some space.

I was sitting in the living room, watching cartoons as usual, when Harmony crossed my mind. She never called me back after I had called her that night. I knew she was probably still upset with me, but me not being at the hotel when she came that morning was old now. I missed her and I just wanted to hear her voice, so I picked up my phone and decided to try my luck with her.

"What's up?" she asked as soon as she answered.

"Hey, Mony. I'm so glad you answered. I missed you."

"Hey, Elle, and yeah, I've thought about you some, too."

"Are you still mad at me?"

"No, I've been over that shit. I've just been staying to myself and vibing with only a few."

"Oh, I understand."

"Yeah, I didn't mean to shut you out like that, but I felt like it was necessary. You know how I am. I don't like being lied to. That bullshit pisses me off. So, when you lied and wasn't where you were supposed to be, I was good off of you for a while. But you're my sister so that could only last for so long. That's why I'm glad you called," she said and then started choking.

"Are you okay?"

"I'm straight. This weed just strong as hell. Damn, this that gas pack."

"Say what?"

"Elle, stop playing, you know I smoke. Don't get to acting now. We just got back cool," she said and laughed. I knew she smoked. I was just hoping she had stopped. But, who am I to judge? I still got that cocaine in my room in that drawer. Now that I think about it. I need to get rid of that stuff.

"I'm chilling," I said, trying to sound like my sister.

"Bitch, I'm dying! Don't you ever say that shit again, with your proper ass!" Mony screamed into the phone after she had stopped laughing.

"It's not that funny, Mony!"

"Yeah the fuck it is! Ya girl say she chilling. Hell to the fuck no!"

"Whatever," I said, laughing myself now. "When is the last time you talked to Nova?" I asked because Nova hadn't said anything about Mony since she had been here.

"I haven't and I don't plan to!"

"Y'all into it or something? I know she hasn't said anything about you since she's been living with me."

"Wait a minute! Wait one damn minute!"

"What is it, Harmony?"

"I know damn well you don't have Nova living with you, Elle."

"Yeah, she needed somewhere to stay after her and Sean broke up."

"When the fuck did that happen?"

"Not too long ago."

"Get that bitch out of your shit! She's sneaky as fuck and I don't trust her!"

"Harmony, calm down, please."

"Elle, you need to listen to what the fuck I'm telling you. I know that's our sister and all, but Nova is fucked up in the head. I never noticed it before, but something is off when it comes to her. I could see it all in her face the last time I saw her. She's conniving as fuck. If she's doing what I think she is, I'm going to kill the bitch and I let her know that the last time I saw her."

"What do you think she is doing?"

"Don't worry about it, Elle. Just get her out of your shit."

"I can't do that. I won't do that."

"Look, I'm trying to look out for you. I would tell you more, but I know you're sensitive and I don't have the facts. So, I'm not going to get you upset off of something I'm thinking. I may be wrong and I hope I am, but you never know. That's why I just want you to listen to me right now."

"Well, I'm sorry, but I can't. Especially when I don't even know what's going on. Thanks for being concerned though."

"Whatever. But look, I'll get up with you later. I'm trying to finish this blunt on up. I love you and keep your eyes open."

"I love you too, Mony," I said and hung up the phone. I sat there for a while wondering what on this earth Harmony was talking about. I finally shrugged it off and started back watching my cartoons.

CHAPTER 20

CASANOVA

The last few months haven't been anything but hell for me. Charles and Elle were making me sick with all of their lovey dovey bullshit. I knew I was going to have some problems on my hand when I heard them in their room talking.

At first I wasn't that worried about them fixing their relationship. I figured Charles was just telling Elle what she wanted to hear, even though the shit had pissed me off. I still tried to let it go and hope for the best. Well, the best didn't come. The worst came.

All they do is pay attention to each other. The shit made me so mad when it first started happening. I was so pissed that I started taking my anger out on the both of them. Of course, Elle tried to talk to me numerous times about what was wrong, but I didn't have shit to say to her about it. I would tell her I was straight and keep it pushing.

I refuse to move out though. That's not going to happen. I moved in to get Charles and I'm not leaving until he's mine. I just have to have him. That's why I needed for my mom to come home. I needed her as a distraction like yesterday. But, she told me a month ago that she wasn't coming.

So, guess what I did? I cut her ass the fuck off. If she didn't want to help me, there was no need for me to continue to talk to her. I mean, no, she didn't know the real reason I wanted her here, but the fake reason should have been enough to get her here. That's why I have been ignoring her phone calls lately.

I've also been sick as hell lately. It's gotten so bad that I had no choice but to come to the doctor today. I didn't want to come alone, so I asked London to come with me. Well, London drove because I didn't even feel like doing that. I had peed in a cup and now I was sitting in my own little room with London. We were waiting for the doctor to come in and take a look at me. A few more minutes passed by before we heard a tap at the door.

"Come in," I called out.

"Good morning, Ms. Banks. How are you?" the doctor came in and asked.

"Not good," I said and rolled my eyes. I mean, what kind of question was that? I wasn't sitting here for nothing.

"Well, talk to me about what's going on."

"I feel weak 24/7. I'm always nauseous and I can't eat shit without throwing it back up. I don't know what's going on because I've never felt like this before."

"Interesting... Give me a minute, Ms. Banks. I think I know what's going on with you," he said and headed for the door.

"You think? Don't you need to be drawing blood so we can get to the bottom of this. Then you can prescribe me some medicine and I can be on my way."

"Just a minute," the doctor said smiling and walked on out of my room.

"That was rude! It already took him forever to come in here. Now, he done left right back out," London said.

"That's what I'm saying! I don't have time for this, I'm ready to go."

"Ms. Banks?" the doctor tapped on the door and asked before coming back into the room.

"Yes."

"I have the results back from your urine test and it looks like you're pregnant."

"Say what?"

"You're pregnant! Congratulations!"

"Oh my God! London, do you hear that?"

"Yes," she said flatly and gave me a look. I ignored her and started listening to the doctor because he had started back talking.

***

"So, who's the baby daddy?" London asked as we headed to get something to eat. We had finished up at the doctor's office not too long ago. We found out that I am exactly a few months pregnant, which means I must've gotten pregnant the very last time I had sex with Charles. It had either happened at the hotel that night or in the shower. I don't really care when though. I'm pregnant and that's all that matters. Charles was about to have it coming.

I never really wanted to just tell Elle out the blue. I wanted her to catch us in the act, but that was impossible. Now that I'm pregnant though, I'm going to make Charles tell her out of his own mouth. I can't wait to see the look on her face, but first, I need to make him want to be with me again. Destroying his and Elle's relationship will be pointless if I don't get him in the end.

"Who do you think, London?" I asked annoyed.

"I don't know, but I hope not Charles."

"Well, hope again because he is. I thought we talked about you being on my side when it came to this?"

"We did, but it's just so wrong, girl."

"I don't give a fuck!"

"Nova, calm down. I hate to say this, but I think you should get an abortion."

"You think I should get a what?!"

"An abortion. I mean, let's be serious, if you have this baby, Elle is going to find out that you and Charles have been messing around. You don't want to hurt her like that, Nova. Think about your family!"

"Fuck them and fuck you! I'm going to have this baby and no one is going to stop me! You know what, pull the fuck over!"

"Just calm down. I'll take you to get something to eat and then I'll take you home. But I'm not going to just let you out in the middle of the street."

"Let me out! Let me out!" I yelled and started beating on her. She swerved into the other lane, causing the person in that lane to slam on their brakes. I didn't give a fuck though. I just wanted out of her damn car. I don't even know why I bothered giving her another chance.

"Are you fucking crazy?!" she screamed as she pulled over into the median.

"Bitch, I might be!" I yelled as I got out and slammed her door. She sped off and didn't look back. Crazy how the tables had turned and now I was the one without a ride. My phone started ringing and I answered it without looking.

"WHAT IS IT?" I asked, pissed, not giving a fuck about who

was on the phone.

"Hey, sweetie," my mom said. Fuck! I should have looked to see who was calling.

"Mom, what do you want?"

"I've been trying to get in touch with you, but you haven't been answering your phone. I wanted to tell you that I had changed my mind about coming. Since I couldn't get you on the phone to tell you, I decided to fly on in and surprise you." Her words instantly cheered me up.

"Oh my God! Really? Where are you? When will you get here?"

"We just landed and I'm at the airport. That's why I'm glad you answered, or I would have had to stay in a hotel today."

"I'm coming to get you, Mommy! Stay put," I said and hung up the phone. Then I googled the number to a taxi and called right away. My mom decided to come at the perfect time and now it was about to be game time!

CHAPTER 21

HARMONY

These last few months haven't been anything but perfect for me, minus the stalking ass cops. They were still watching my every fucking move. I'm pretty sure they are getting pissed by now though, because I haven't been doing a damn thing but spending all of my time with Kelly.

The last few months with him have been great. We're not official yet, but I feel like we're close to it. He spends a lot of time at my place now, and I don't mind at all. Everything just seems so easy with him. Nothing is forced. Not even the conversation between us. I knew he was a great guy before, but I could really see it now since I'm no longer blinded by AK's bullshit.

Kelly is a real fucking man. I don't say that because he pays all of my bills either, even though I really don't need for him too. Especially since he isn't as big as AK. He's just an ordinary weed man. But don't get me wrong, he's making some money. He got a few blocks on lock, out in his city, and they keep his pockets loaded.

Anyway, what I mean when I say he's a real man is he does manly shit. He cooks for me, he runs my bathwater, he doesn't mind sitting and just talking with me about my day, and he was still holding out on the dick. He was serious about not giving me none. It was driving me crazy, but I liked where things were going with him.

Today he's taking me out for lunch, and I'm so excited. We haven't been out anywhere together yet, so I'm past ready for this. Kelly is really taking things slow with me. I think he's still trying to read me and trying to make sure that I'm over AK, but he doesn't have to worry when it comes to that.

"Hello?" I said after I had answered my ringing phone.

"Bring yo' ass on, girl," Kelly said.

"Why you ain't come up, crazy?"

"Because I'm hungry as hell and if I came up, it would have motivated you to take your sweet time getting ready."

"Shut up! Here I come," I said laughing a little bit. His ass is so fucking silly.

"Bout time," Kelly said as soon as I slid into his passenger seat.

"Ain't nobody tell you to sit down here in the car for however long you've been out here. Should have come up, smart ass."

"Owee, I can't wait to fix that smart ass mouth of yours."

"Fix it because I've been waiting for months now," I said and smiled at him.

"Nasty ass. I'mma fix it sooner than you know," he said and

smirked at me.

"Lies."

We pulled up to the restaurant and the valet parked Kelly's car. We were seated as soon as we walked in. Apparently, Kelly had made reservations. I was cheesing hard as fuck already and we had just got here. The fact that Kelly's hood ass took out time to do something this sweet for me melted my heart.

Kelly and I had eaten and now we were just sipping on our drinks as we scanned through the dessert menu. Well, I scanned through the dessert menu because Kelly didn't want anything. He assured me that I could take my time though, so I was doing just that.

"Ma'am, are you ready to order?" the waitress walked over and asked for the third time since I'd been holding the dessert menu. She thought she was slick. Her ass had been switching all around ever since we had gotten here. Seriously, when we first were seated, she was just walking regular. But as soon as she spotted Kelly, she started trying to swing them hips as she walked. She looked a fucking mess, but I doubt she knew that.

"No, I'm not, damn. I'll let you know when I'm the fuck ready," I snapped and dismissed her ass with a wave of my hand. She was being mad disrespectful and I didn't appreciate that shit. So I got nasty with her ass, hoping she would get a fucking clue.

Because if she switches her ass over here one more time without me calling her over here, I'm going to beat the bitch.

"Stop being mean, Harmony," Kelly said, laughing. "They gone spit in yo' shit."

"I wish they would! I'll turn this whole damn restaurant out!"

"You rough, girl." I didn't respond to Kelly, I just started back looking over the menu. After I had decided what I wanted, I waved my hand for the waitress to come over. That bitch looked me dead in my face and then turned her head like she didn't see me. I slid my chair back so I could get up because this hoe was about to get it!

"Chill," Kelly said and held up his hand to wave the waitress over. She came over right away and gave me a little smile. I swear I was about to kill me a bitch. I told Kelly what I wanted and then he told the waitress, but not before warning her not to spit in my shit. He swore he was going to eat some too, but I know he didn't want me to have to go off in this bitch.

My dessert came out 10 minutes later. The waitress was still trying to be funny, so instead of placing it in front of me, she set the plate in front of Kelly. Then she rolled her eyes and walked off. I pulled the plate in front of me and started eating it right away. Kelly took a few bites.

"This good as fuck!" I said as I continued to eat.

"Harmony."

"What, Kelz? Damn, you see I'm trying to eat."

"Look at me."

"In a minute!" I fussed.

"Look, now." I dropped my spoon loudly and looked at Kelly with an annoyed look, but that look was replaced with a look of surprise. Kelly was sitting in front of me with an opened box that displayed a gorgeous ass ring.

"Nigga, I know you not proposing," I said, never taking my eyes off of the ring.

"Ain't nobody proposing to your ass, crazy girl, but I do want you to be mine. This here is a promise ring. So what do you say? Be my queen?"

"Hold on. What you promising, nigga?" I asked, because I just needed to know before I accepted his fly ass ring and decided to be his girl. I like him and everything and I know he's the one for me, but he had better make this shit good.

"I promise to cherish you like the diamond in the rough that you are. I promise to always be here for you. I promise to protect you. I promise to hold you down at all times and I promise to love you like no other," he said and then winked at me.

"Give me the ring then, dawg," I said cheesing. He slid the ring on my finger and leaned across the table to kiss me. After we kissed, I spotted the waitress staring at us. I smirked at her ass this time as we got up and got ready to go. Kelly placed a couple of hundreds on the table and then we made our way outside.

The valet brought us the car right away. We hopped in and headed back to my place. I looked at Kelly the whole entire ride. This nigga is smooth. I give him that. We pulled up to my place and got out. I looked across the street and there sat the cops, of course. It took everything in me not to stick their asses a birdie. I did look at them and cock an eyebrow though. Then Kelly and I headed upstairs to my apartment.

Once we were inside, we went straight to my room. Kelly started rolling up while I changed my clothes. When I was done changing, I sat on the bed beside Kelly and stared at my pretty ass ring. AK's cheap ass had never given me a ring and we dated for years. That's that clown activity.

"I saw yo' ass down there fucking with them cops," Kelly said smiling, and then lit the blunt.

"I wasn't doing shit."

"Yeah, whatever. Gon' make me have to body one of them motherfuckers all because you want to fuck with them."

"Is that a problem?" I asked laughing.

"Hell nah, as long as they stay across that damn street, they straight though."

"Word," I said and took the blunt from Kelly.

When we finished smoking, Kelly left, but not before telling me how happy he was that I was his. I thought that shit was sweet. I hated that he had to go though. Now I was left all alone with my thoughts. I couldn't help but to replay the conversation I had with Elle a couple of months ago.

Nova living with her just didn't sound right. Because for one, she has a condo that she could have stayed at. Two, she said her and Sean had broken up and that just didn't sound right at all. Nova loved that man's money, so I can't imagine what happened to make her let him go. Everything just sounded wrong. I couldn't prove she had shit going on with Charles, but I felt like she did.

I tried to make Elle get that sneaky bitch out of her house, but she wasn't going for it. I had no choice but to let it be because I didn't want to say anything to Elle. Then if I was just tripping, Elle would be hurt for nothing and her relationship would probably suffer from my accusations. I wasn't trying to cause shit like that. Therefore, I stayed in my own lane like I will continue to do.

CHAPTER 22

NADIA

A lot of shit has changed in the past few months. Okay, not that much has changed, but a few things have. AK is living with me now. He still hasn't committed to me though. That's starting to piss me off. I'm trying to hold my tongue on the whole situation though. I'm even trying to be patient, but fuck, I'm sick of this. I just knew after Harmony and AK were over that I would be next up. But, that was far from the truth.

Then to top shit off, AK had the nerve to treat me like shit. I mean he never had really treated me that great, but it was worse now. All he does is fuss and complain about everything that I do. I was excited for him to move in here when he first mentioned it. Now, I just want him gone. I think things were better when we had our separate places. I can't kick him out though. I mean, he is the one paying my rent after all.

One thing I don't understand is why I'm still working. When he was with Harmony, she didn't have to work. She just went on them stupid ass runs for him and he blessed her pockets. I wanted for him to bless mine, shit. So I walked in my room, where he was laid out chilling, and brought up the subject of making runs.

"What do your people have to do when they go on those runs for you?" I asked as I climbed in the bed beside him.

"Didn't you used to go with Harmony when she would do it?" he asked, mean mugging me.

"Yes."

"Okay, then. Therefore, you know what be going on. Don't come in here asking stupid questions and getting on my fucking nerves, Nadia."

"I'm just asking. I thought maybe I could start doing it for you. I'm sick of working at McDonald's and I need more money."

"Yo' ass better get un-sick of it because you ain't doing a damn thing for me, snitch ass."

"Look, you need to let that shit go!"

"I'm not letting shit go! Harmony was in a fucked up situation all because of you."

"You say that like you haven't caused her to be in a fucked up situation before!"

"That ain't none of your damn business!"

"It is my business because you coming on to me is what started all of this bullshit."

"I don't remember you trying to stop shit, Nadia."

"I did too, and you know it! So save the shit, and you need to stop taking your anger out on me! It's not my fault Harmony won't take you back!"

"It is your fucking fault. Should have kept your fucking mouth closed. You an ignorant ass bitch, man. I swear you is."

"Why the fuck you move in here with me then if that's how you feel? I'm not some kind of rebound, AK!"

"You is a fucking rebound. That's all you good for! Either that or being a side bitch!"

"You know what—fuck you! I've given you nothing but my all, and this is how you're going to treat me?"

"Man, I ain't got time for this shit!" he yelled and stood up.

"Where are you going?!"

"Out!"

Just like that, he was gone. That's what I meant by him treating me like shit. He seriously just exploded on me for nothing. All he had to do is tell me no. But no, he couldn't do that. He wanted to be extra and do the most. I swear he's working my damn nerves.

I got up and went to the kitchen to get me some orange juice. After I was done drinking my juice, I heard my phone ringing in my room. I took off down the hall thinking it could be AK wanting to apologize. Only thing is, it wasn't.

"What is it?" I answered the phone, aggravated.

"Where are you?"

"Home, why?"

"We still haven't been able to get shit on Ms. Banks. We need your help or all of this shit is going to pass us by and she's going to be free!"

"She's already free! Like I said before, I don't understand why y'all let her out! I'm sick of this shit. Now, I tried to help y'all, but ain't shit more I can do for y'all!"

"You can get your ass down here and tell me who this guy is she's always with. We can use him!"

"I told you I didn't know!"

"No, you said you probably didn't know! You never even saw who I'm talking about."

"And I'm not going to! Look, y'all fucked up, but you still made a drug bust. Y'all might as well just let the shit go!" I yelled and hung up the phone. I was sick of his ass bothering me. That shit was so old now and I no longer cared to be bothered. Hell, Harmony wasn't a problem of mine anymore. Not that much. I just need for AK to stop bringing her up! I was sick of hearing about her because I was starting to miss my friendship with her.

My phone started ringing again and I ignored it. I know it ain't nobody but that damn officer calling me back. He was going to make me go down the fucking street and slap his baldheaded ass, bothering me and shit when I clearly don't have time. All of this shit was really starting to stress me out.

CHAPTER 23

CARRIE

"Put y'all shoes on so I can take y'all over to your grandma's house!" I yelled out to my kids. Their bad asses hadn't been doing shit but getting on my nerves since school had been out. That's why I'm glad it's almost time for the shit to start back.

All of my kids came running into the living room with their shoes in their hands. Well, all of them accept for Cam. He had called his daddy the day after I had worn his little ass out. Got on the phone telling him everything that I had said. I didn't give a fuck though. The only thing that killed me was when Cam showed up at my house talking about he was coming to get his son.

He only came to get him to prove a fucking point. He ain't want his kids living with him. If he did, he would have been brought it up to me. He just wanted to shut me up for once. That spiteful bastard. I would whoop Lil' Cam's ass all over again if I could. When his daddy gets tired of fucking around with him, his little ass is gone be right back here looking stupid! *Fucking kids!*

"Chez, put your shoes on and then help your sisters! I told y'all to put them on, not come in here with them in your hands!"

"Okay, Mama!" he answered and done exactly what he was told. Chez was my heart out of all of my kids. He was bad as hell, but he was obedient.

After they all had their shoes on, we headed out the door and walked next door to my mama's apartment. I tried to go on in, but of course, her old ass had the fucking door locked. I started banging on the door like the fucking police because she needed to hurry the hell up. She finally came to the door and opened it a few seconds later.

"Hey, babies. Y'all come on in," my momma said as she bent down to kiss my kids on their cheeks.

"Hey, Grammy!" they all yelled at once before running on into her place.

"I'll be back later, Ma. I got shit to do."

"Alright, Ari. I love you," she said as she continued to stand in the doorway.

"Yeah, love ya," I said, before taking off back to my apartment.

It was finally quiet and I could hear myself thinking for once. I was sitting at the kitchen table looking through a hair magazine. I had somebody coming soon to get their head done. I usually could pick up on how to do a hairstyle by just seeing a picture. That's why I liked to look through these magazines before I did somebody's head.

I had recently changed my hair up after I saw a picture of a hairstyle I liked in this exact magazine. I no longer had that bob;

instead, I had given myself a bad ass Vixen Sew-In. So, now my hair was black and long, and flowing down my back. Okay, I mean my weave was black and flowing down my back. I had paid for it though, so that made it mine, shit. I heard a knock at the door so I jumped up to get it.

"What's up? You busy?" AK stood at my door and asked.

"Yes."

"Man, no you not. Let me come in for a lil' bit. I'll let you suck on my dick or some shit. I know how you like doing that."

"Akeem, get the fuck on!" I yelled and slammed my door shut. I had become tired of Akeem. All he did was lie and fuck around. It took me a while to realize he didn't want me. All he wanted to do was fuck me and tell me lies. Plus, after that night I had fucked with Nadia at work about him, I went home and thought about some shit. She was so fucking pressed that she had got mad as hell at my words. Funny how things work out, but that shit opened my eyes. Nadia was in love with AK too. I thought she was pathetic at first, but then I realized I was just as pathetic as her ass.

Akeem didn't want to settle down with nobody. All he wanted to do was fuck around. He was nothing but a lil' ass boy, and I didn't want shit to do with him anymore. That's why I had started back talking to Cynthia's daddy. Like I said before, Randall is a complete sweetheart and he will do anything when it comes to me and my kids.

I don't know why I even let him go. He's a real fucking man and that's what me and my kids needed in our lives. I was interrupted from my thoughts when I heard another knock at my door. I quickly went to open the door, ready to give AK a piece of my mind.

"Hey, girl! Sorry I'm late. My baby daddy had got to tripping before I left the house. He started playing acting like he ain't want to give me the money to get my hair done and shit," this girl named Kyla said. She worked at McDonald's with me and Nadia.

"Girl, I thought you was my damn baby daddy. I was about to go in on your ass."

"Shit, which one? You got like a thousand," she said laughing as she came on into my apartment.

"Shut the hell up! Kyla, where ya hair at, honey?" I asked when I noticed she didn't have any hair with her.

"Girl, I ain't have enough money for it. I only got enough to pay you. I told you my baby daddy was tripping."

"Pay me to do what, child? Comb yo' bald head? 'Cause I can't do shit with this without no weave."

"I mean, you do hair or whatever, I figured you had something laying around here. What kind of hairstylist is you?"

"Bitch, the door!" I yelled and pointed at the door. She had really just tried it coming in here with that bullshit.

"Can't you just braid it or something, Carrie?"

"I can't do a fucking thing! Now get the fuck out before I toss you out!"

"You bugging!" she yelled as she made her way to my front door.

"Bitch, and you broke! Get the hell out!"

She had really lost her damn mind. I bet this would be the last time she ever came over here because her ass was officially banned. I don't know what the fuck she smoking on, but she better get a grip. That shit right there didn't make no damn sense. I thought about going back to get my kids, but I decided against it. I needed to relax for now. That damn girl had me heated.

I could have been doing somebody else's head instead of fucking around with her. Baldheaded ass bitch. Then she thought I was going to put some braids in her hair. What the fuck ever!

CHAPTER 24

NOELLE

Today was the last day of my online class, and I had passed it with flying colors, like I was supposed to the first time. I was so happy and excited that I had got this class out of the way. Now, I wouldn't have to deal with Professor Black anymore. I hadn't heard from him these last few months and I was glad.

I didn't need anything destroying my good spirits. Charles had me on cloud nine these days. Believe it or not, we had started trying to have sex every two weeks. It wasn't much, but it was a step in the right direction and Charles seemed to enjoy it. His face had lit up like it was Christmas morning when I suggested it.

I told him that I eventually wanted to do it more, but every two weeks was the perfect start for me. He wouldn't have cared if I had said every three weeks. I guess he was just glad to be getting sex more than three times a year. I finally realized that, that could drive a man crazy. That's why I was doing my best to satisfy Charles. I hadn't had any complaints from him yet.

I had still been job hunting, only to come up empty handed time and time again. Everybody swore you needed experience. All I've been wondering is how am I supposed to get experience when I need experience JUST TO GET EXPERIENCE. That was so messed up to me, and the logic behind it didn't make sense. Like, who comes up with this stuff? They can't possibly be thinking these things through.

Anyway, Charles had just got home from work and we were in the kitchen cooking dinner together. We haven't cooked together in forever. That's something we used to do when we first started dating, so I was happy we were getting back to the way things used to be. We were cooking a seafood meal. There was fish, crawfish, shrimp, crab legs, lobster, and so much more.

"What is that terrible smell?" I heard Nova come through the front door and ask.

"Don't come in here bitching, Nova! We not in the mood for it," Charles said and I swatted him with my towel. "What? If I don't say nothing to her she gone come in here and suck all of the air out of this damn room."

"Charles, leave her alone," I said as I wiped my hands off on the hand towel and headed to the living room. When I got in there, I stopped dead in my tracks.

"Elle, I'm glad you came in here! We have a guest!" Nova said excitedly.

"I'm no guest! I'm just your mom, so don't worry about me. I'll make myself comfortable."

"Does... does Dad know you're here?" I asked, just staring at her. I hadn't saw this woman since I was 13-years-old. I knew her, but I didn't know her.

"Of course not. He doesn't need to know either. I'm here to see my girls, not him," my mom said as she looked around my condo. She walked over to me and hugged me tightly. I just gave her a pat on the back.

"Charles!" I yelled.

"Yes, baby?" he came flying into the living room and asked. "Who the hell is this? Nova, who you done brought into our home without our permission?" he asked once he spotted my mom. I'm surprised he didn't see the resemblance.

"No need for permission. You must be Elle's little boyfriend," my mom said.

"I mean, yeah, okay. I see we all know who I am. So, who the hell are you, lady?"

"Elle's mother," she said tight lipped as she looked down her nose at Charles. We looked a lot alike, but she acted like Nova. Well, I guess Nova acted like her.

"That's funny. I've never seen you before. No one talks about you either. Matter of fact, I don't think I've ever heard anything about you and I work with Elle's dad. I thought you was dead or some shit," Charles said flat out.

"Charles, sweetie, can you get my mom's things and get her set up in a guest room downstairs? I'll finish up the food," I said, dismissing Charles quickly because he didn't seem to be a fan of my mom. I think it was her snobbish attitude that rubbed him the wrong way. He grabbed her things and headed out the living room. I walked back to the kitchen so I could finish cooking. Of course, Nova followed, right along with my mom. They sat at the kitchen table and chatted amongst themselves.

Twenty minutes later, the food was done and we all were seated at the table. Nova didn't want any of the seafood and ate a salad instead. My mom was eating the seafood up though. That snobbish attitude had disappeared while she ate. I was trying to chew up my food when my mom decided to speak.

"So, when can I see Harmony?" she asked, causing me to choke. I didn't like my mom because of what she had did. I was hurt because of it. But Harmony *hated* her because of what she did. She was dead to her, so I knew she would be the last person that Harmony wanted to see.

"Somewhere out in the hood, Mom. I told you that's where she stayed," Nova said.

"My God, what is she doing in the slums?" my mom asked.

"The who?" Charles asked looking up from his plate.

"The slums!" my mom reiterated.

"I'm going to have to excuse myself," Charles said and got up from the table. He put his plate in the dishwasher and then he was gone.

"What's his problem?" my mom asked.

"Charles is from the hood. He may not look like it, but he is. He's a working man now so he stays away from there, but it's still a sensitive subject for him," I let her know.

"Oh, okay. Well, he should be glad he found something better and got away from there."

"I guess," I said, as I got up and put my plate in the dishwasher also. I was about to head out of the kitchen until my mom stopped me.

"Noelle, I would like us all to have breakfast in the morning. Do you think you can get in touch with Harmony to let her know?"

"I'll try," I said and then sped out of the kitchen. *God, no!* I thought to myself. A breakfast with all of us didn't sound good. I went to my bedroom and picked up my phone. I decided I would call Harmony right away while Charles was in the shower.

"Yo?" she answered after a couple of rings.

"Hey, I hate to bother you. But, umm, do you want to have breakfast in the morning?"

"I don't see why not. Why you sound like that, Elle?"

"Like… what?"

"Nervous!"

"Mony, mom is here and Nova brought her."

"Wait, you say what?"

"You heard me right. She wants us all to go out and have breakfast together in the morning," I said quickly.

"Oh, so this is her shit you inviting me to?"

"Yes."

"I'm not coming!"

"Harmony, please! I need you to come. I can't escape her, she's staying here."

"That's your fault, Elle. If you had put Nova out like I told you to, you wouldn't be going through this right now."

"I know. I know. Can you please just come?"

"I'll think about it," she said and then hung up the phone.

I knew then that I was going to have to be strong in more than a few areas, because maybe Nova was a problem like Harmony had said. Maybe I should have kicked her out. I couldn't bring myself to be that person though, but I would watch Nova a little bit more. She was the one that told me to stop being weak. But, I couldn't help but to feel like she was one of the main ones walking all over me.

Charles was in the bed now and I was ready to cuddle up with him and get some rest, but I had one more phone call to make before I did.

CHAPTER 25

CASANOVA

I woke up this morning feeling good as hell. My mom was here and I could already tell she was going to be the perfect distraction. Then, to top things off, I'm pregnant with Charles's baby. I felt like everything was once again back in my favor and I planned on milking the shit out of this situation. They thought they had one upped me. I know they did.

But, they were on my playing field now. Just call me Nova... The Puppet Master, because I was about to start pulling strings and controlling shit around here. I knew my beauty could only get me so far, so now it was time for me to start using my head.

I had just got out of the shower and now I was sliding into some of my expensive threads. I matched up my purse and pumps and then I was ready to go. I headed out of my room and made my way up the stairs.

When I got up there, I saw Charles and Elle standing in front of the front door, kissing. I loudly cleared my throat and then strutted into the living room, making sure to click my heels every step of the way. They abruptly stopped kissing and looked at me. Charles looked pissed and I couldn't read the look on Elle's face, but I definitely could read it last night when she saw my mom. She looked like she had seen a fucking ghost. If she could have disappeared I bet she would have. I found it all hilarious. Then mom just put the icing on the cake when she started talking. I see where I got my cleverness and sass from.

"I'm sorry, Nova. We didn't see you there," Elle said. Only, she didn't look like she was really sorry.

"Y'all never do," I shot back.

"This is our shit, so quite frankly, we don't give a fuck. We will do what the fuck we want to do, when we want to do it. It doesn't matter if you in the room or not. You don't pay no bills here," Charles said looking at me with disgust in his eyes. If he knew what was best for him he would shut his mouth.

"My oh my… I hope you don't kiss your mother with that mouth, boy," my mother said walking into the room. Charles didn't acknowledge her at all. He kissed Elle one last time and then he left. Elle just stood there for a second, smiling to herself, like she approved of Charles's actions.

"Shall we go?" I spoke up and asked.

"Wait, I need to send the location to Mony and let her know that we are headed out. Where are we going?" Elle asked. My mom told her what she needed to know and then we proceeded out the door.

Elle drove us to the restaurant. I don't think she wanted our company in her car either, but my mom wasn't having that. She walked straight over to her car and hopped in the front seat. I slid in the back and watched as Elle drove the entire ride. If she didn't want us to ride with her she sure didn't show it. We went inside of the fancy little breakfast place and took a seat. We ordered our drinks and waited for Harmony to show up, although I was hoping she wouldn't.

CHAPTER 26

HARMONY

I woke up to the sound of Kelly snoring. I found snoring so irritating, so I nudged the fuck out of him. He stopped snoring, but he didn't wake up. He had come back over in the middle of the night. I was glad too, because I just couldn't get to sleep without him in the bed with me.

I turned on my side and closed my eyes so that I could get back to sleep. That was ruined when I heard my phone ding. I told myself not to check the text, but I reached over and grabbed my phone off of the nightstand anyway. I saw the text was from Elle and regretted picking up my phone instantly.

She had sent me the location to where they were heading to. I didn't want to go, but I felt like I needed to. I had missed Elle and I felt like I had shut her out for long enough. I knew she was going to need me so I got up. I was a little pissed though, because I told her to kick Nova out. If she had, she wouldn't have even had to see Angela's face.

Angela is my mom's name, but I don't fuck with her like that so that's why I call her by her first name most of the time. I hadn't seen this bitch since I was 14 and quite fucking frankly, I had planned on keeping it that way. I didn't need or want her in my life. I don't even know why the fuck she is here. She hasn't been worried about us, so what possessed her to bring her ass this way.

I pulled up to the restaurant almost 40 minutes late and hopped out my car. I went into the restaurant and spotted them in the back. I slowly made my way over to them. When I approached the table, Nova and Angela were talking and laughing. Elle sat off to the side playing with her straw. I took a seat beside her and squeezed her knee, just to reassure her everything was going to be fine. She looked at me and I saw something different in her. She looked… confident.

"Sweetie, I'm glad you could join us!" Angela said excitedly.

"What's up?" I shot back.

"Why don't you come and give your mother a hug. I haven't seen you in forever."

"You straight," I said back.

"I'm what?" she asked, looking confused.

"You not getting a damn hug. I'm good," I said sternly. I refused to sit in here and be fake with this bitch. So, sitting and smiling in her face was never in my plans.

"You watch your mouth, young lady. I am your mother and you will treat me as that!"

"Angela, I'mma let you in on a little secret. YOUR ASS AIN'T BEEN NO MOTHER TO ME SINCE I WAS 14! SO YOU

CAN FALL THE FUCK BACK WITH THAT BULLSHIT! I'MMA TELL YA TRIFLING ASS THIS ONE TIME AND ONE TIME ONLY. I AM NOT THE MOTHERFUCKING ONE, SO PLEASE DON'T TRY ME!" I yelled because somebody needed to get her ass straight, and I was the right one to do it.

"HARMONY MELODY BANKS!" she yelled back covering her mouth.

"Ladies!" a guy yelled as he approached our table. I didn't turn to look at him because I was too busy giving Angela's ass the death stare. Elle hopped up out of her seat.

"Daddy! I'm so glad you're here," she said and I turned to look at my daddy who was looking right at my mom.

"I'm sorry, but we're going to have to ask you all to leave," a waiter came over to our table and said.

"Shit, gladly. Y'all ain't doing me nothing but a fucking favor," I said getting up. "Get the fuck out the way!" I yelled at the waiter. He wanted us gone, but was still standing here in the way. He quickly turned on his heels and walked away.

"Don't," my dad said to me as he grabbed my arm while I was trying to walk away. "Let's all go over to my place and we can talk about all of this."

"I don't have a damn thing to talk about with that bitch!" I said, and shot Angela a look. Then I proceeded on out of the restaurant.

Them motherfuckers had lost their damn minds. The shit they were trying to do was long overdue and I wasn't for it no more. There wasn't no hope for this fucking family. All hope flew out the window when my mom walked out on us. But, oh now they wanted to sit down and fucking kumbaya. In other words, they wanted to try to sit down and make the situation peaceful. I wasn't going for that shit. I got in my car and sped straight back to my place.

When I walked into my place, Kelly was sitting on the couch smoking. I walked over to him and reached for the blunt. He gave it to me and I hit it right away. I inhaled deeply before blowing the smoke out. Then I passed it back to Kelly as I took a seat in his lap.

"Damn, you straight? Who I need to go fuck up?" he asked and I laughed. "You laughing and I'm serious. What's wrong with you?"

"Just some bullshit. You know I told you I was leaving this morning to go have breakfast with my folks?" I asked and he nodded his head. "Well, that shit went bad fast. That's all."

"Damn."

"Yup, but forget that. What we getting into today?"

"I'm trying to get into you. Shit, you mine now and I got plans to tear that pussy up. You been talking all of that shit, so you know I'm about to punish yo ass, right?"

"Oh my God," I said blushing.

"God can't help you now. Get your ass up and get in that room!" he said and slapped the fuck out my thigh. I hit his blunt one more time before doing what I was told.

When I got in my room, I laid across my bed and waited for Kelly. He walked in with his shirt in his hand, looking sexy as fuck. He threw it on the floor and then walked over to the bottom of the bed. He grabbed me by my ankles and pulled me down, then he started literally ripping my clothes off. Like, this motherfucker had actually torn my shit up to get it off of me. He smiled at me cockily before snatching me up off of my bed.

He picked me up and I wrapped my legs around his waist. He walked over to the wall and slammed me up against it roughly. He then started sucking on my neck hard as hell. He started sucking all on my chest and titties. I knew he was leaving hickies everywhere, but I did not care. He pulled on my weave roughly and I almost stopped everything right there, because I did not fuck around with niggas pulling on my weave. That was a no! I paid money for this shit!

Nevertheless, his roughness was turning me on, so I let it slide. It didn't take much longer before he had slammed me back on the bed. He reached in his pocket and pulled a condom out, before sliding his joggers off and slipping the condom on. He licked my center a few times and I started gushing for him right away. I guess he couldn't take much more of seeing how wet I was, so he sucked up my juices quickly before ramming himself inside of me. I moaned out in pleasure and pain. He was not playing when he said he was going to punish my ass!

CHAPTER 27

PROFESSOR BLACK

I haven't thought about anything or anyone but Noelle these last couple of months. Since school was out now, I haven't been able to see her, and God knows I needed to see her. I thought I would have seen her when she saw her test results, but I didn't. She didn't come to me like I was once sure she would.

That bothered me because I craved to see her face. I felt like I was going to explode if I didn't get to her soon. I guess she was still upset about me having her clothes. But the look on her face when she saw them sitting on my desk that day was priceless.

I had heard that she filed a complaint on me and I didn't like that shit at all. I had some choice words for her and she was going to hear what I had to say, and she was going to have to face me.

I leaned down and sniffed up the two lines of cocaine that was in front of me. I rubbed my nose and stood up. I walked down the long hallway to my office, unlocked my office door and headed inside. When I got inside, I turned on the lights so I could see her face.

"So you filed a complaint against me, Noelle?" I looked at one of her pictures and asked. "Why would you do that? What did you think was going to happen? ANSWER ME, DAMN IT!" I slammed my fist up against the picture over and over again. "You are mine! You gave yourself to me, remember? Do you fucking remember?" I didn't stop punching the picture until glass was all in my hand from the picture frame.

Blood was dripping from my hand and getting all on my carpet. I didn't care though. I walked out of my office and back down the hall. When I got back into the living room, I picked up my phone and headed back to my office. I sat down at my desk and got on my laptop. After I found what I was looking for, I picked up my cellphone to call Noelle. She had gone long enough without hearing from me.

CHAPTER 28

NOELLE

So, the breakfast with mom was a complete bust. I can't say I minded either. Harmony, had told it like it was and I couldn't have agreed with her more. I am glad Dad showed up though, because there is no telling what else would have gone on.

My mom fussed the entire car ride back to my condo. Now we were inside, sitting around the table drinking tea because that's what she wanted to do. I tried to get out of it, but she swore up and down she needed me. I didn't care too much about her feelings, but I sat down anyway because I didn't want to be rude.

"Can you girls believe your sister? Who is she to talk to me that way? I know what I did was wrong, but I was in love. I was in love and I followed my heart. What's done is done and it's the past. Plus, your father pushed me to it with all of his working. You girls were practically grown. You didn't need me," my mom ignorantly said.

"Excuses," I said, staring at her.

"Excuse me?" she asked.

"I…said…excuses."

"Elle, don't even try to go there with mom," Nova said. I set my cup of tea down and stood up. I walked out of the kitchen and didn't look back. I wasn't in the mood to try to explain myself to them. So instead of sitting there and getting ganged up on in my own house, I went to my room. As soon as I got in my room, I had to use the bathroom. So I went straight there and didn't stop to put my phone down or anything.

After I used the bathroom, I started washing my hands. Of course my phone would start ringing right then. I quickly dried my hands off and answered the phone.

"Hello?"

"Good afternoon, Ms. Banks." I looked down at the phone and kicked myself for answering it.

"What do you want?" I asked right away.

"You. You thought you could get rid of me that easily. Huh? I just knew you were going to come crying to me after I had failed your ass."

"Sorry things didn't turn out your way, Professor."

"Like I said. You thought this all was so easy. Huh? I found out that you put in a complaint against me and decided to retake the class online. Passed it with flying colors... huh?"

"Sure did," I answered knowingly.

"Well know this! I've looked up your address in the school system and I will be seeing you sooner rather than later," he said and then hung up the phone. I stood there in my bathroom, shaking uncontrollably. *What did he mean he had looked up my address and would be seeing me soon?*

Call the police, Elle. Pick up your phone and call the police! I kept thinking to myself. I didn't want to do that though. I didn't want my secrets I've been working so hard to hide and forget, to come up. I had moved past this. I passed that class and thought I wouldn't have to deal with him anymore.

"No! No! I can't take this shit anymore! I can't take it!" I yelled out as I fell out on the bathroom floor. I was banging on the floor and kicking on anything I could get my feet on. I started pulling at my hair as I continued to yell out. "Why can't he just go away! GO AWAY! FUCK HIM!! FUCK HIM! HE WANTS ME, TO RUIN ME! I HATE HIM!"

An hour had passed and I was still in my bathroom sitting on the floor. I was calm now. I had convinced myself that he was making empty threats and that I didn't have anything to worry about. Yet and still, I couldn't snap out of my trance to leave this bathroom.

KNOCK! KNOCK!

"Just... a... umm... wait a second!" I hollered out as I got up off of the floor and fixed my hair and things. When I thought I looked okay again, I opened the door.

"Are you okay? We heard you screaming. An hour had passed by and you still hadn't come out, so I decided to come check on you."

"Oh, I'm fine, Mom. I just had an argument with Charles over the phone… we're good now." I smiled and walked past her out of the bathroom and into my room. I climbed on the bed and looked at my phone.

"Well, alright. But, I was thinking to myself and I know that you and your sister are upset with me. I wanted to throw a small party for you girls and try to get past our differences," she said, looking hopeful. She looked sincere enough so I decided I would give her one last chance.

"That sounds good. When and where do you want to have it?"

"I was thinking we could do it here this Friday."

"Mom, how will we pull that off so quickly? That only gives us a couple of days."

"It's just going to be a small gathering with us, honey."

"Well, okay." My mom smiled at me before leaving my room.

The rest of the day flew by pretty smoothly. I watched TV with my mom some and then we cooked dinner together. Nova had disappeared during the day, but she popped back up when it was time to eat. Charles had to work over so he didn't make it to eat dinner with us. I figured he worked over on purpose, but now we were in the bed facing each other.

"So, how was your day?" I asked.

"It was good. Just long."

"I see that."

"I thought about you all day long though, baby."

"Aww, I thought about you too," I said smiling.

"So, what did I miss today?"

"Everything! Mony completely told my mom off at breakfast this morning. It was so crazy. But my mom wants to have a party here Friday, to try to get us back on track. I'm not too sure if Mony is going to come. I'll have to try my best to get her to."

"Nope!"

"No, what?"

"There isn't going to be a party here!"

"Charles, yes, it is. How about if you invite a couple of friends from your job over? I'll even invite my dad.

"Okay, deal. But, leave your dad out of it. No one is going to come if they know he is." I laughed and kissed his lips.

"I'm going to bed."

"I'm right behind you, baby." We snuggled up close together, but before I went to sleep, I shot Harmony a quick text to tell her about the party.

CHAPTER 29

NADIA

Today was Thursday and I hadn't heard anything else from those fucking cops. He did blow my damn phone up that day I hung up on him though. I was about to put his ass on my block list, but he stopped calling out the blue. Like the shit was dead now so he had might as well let it go.

I haven't heard anything else from AK either. I don't know why he was bugging so bad. Like I said before, all he had to do was tell me no. That would have been the end of that conversation, no matter how badly I wanted to make them runs for him. I was just trying to get some extra money in my pocket, since he wanted to act stingy with his money.

I still don't understand how money wasn't an issue when it came to Harmony. He bought that girl whatever she wanted while still paying her to do those runs. But I can't get nothing out of him outside from paying my rent. He had me fucked up too, because I had been repeatedly calling his ass. It's okay though, because I was about to get up and go knock on Gutta's door.

After I had slid my robe on and tied it shut, I slid my house shoes on and went to the front of my apartment. I opened the door and went across the hall. Then I started banging on Gutta's door. A few seconds passed by before the door was being opened up.

DEJAH RICE

"What's up?" Gutta asked while looking all around.

"Have you seen AK?"

"Yeah, he here. Come on in," he said. I walked into the apartment and Gutta closed the door behind me. The first person I saw when I got inside was London. Instead of going to cuss AK out, I walked over to where she was on the couch to talk to her.

"Hey, London. What you doing over here?" I asked.

"Nothing, smoking with Gutta's ass."

"Oh, I ain't know y'all was cool like that."

"Nadia, mind yo' fucking business, man," Gutta said walking into the living room.

"I'm just saying. Shut up, damn. Anyway, London, when the last time you talked to your bitch ass friend, Nova?" I asked being nosey.

"Tuh, that bitch ain't no friend of mine!"

"Say what? When did this happen?" I asked, sitting down on the couch now.

"Didn't you come over here to see AK? Don't be in here getting comfortable and shit. We trying to smoke," Gutta said.

"Hell, I want to smoke too," I said.

208

"That shit sound personal," Gutta said as he lit a blunt up.

"Whatever. Anyway, London," I said turning my attention back to her.

"Wait, what you over here to see AK for?" London asked.

"That's my man," I said proudly, even though I was stretching the truth. Gutta started laughing and got choked on smoke. *That's what the fuck he gets!*

"No, that's not right. Harmony was with AK, wasn't she?" she asked.

"The keyword is, *was*, sweetheart."

"But, Harmony is your best friend. Why would you do that to her?"

"Not no more."

"Why not? What happened?" she asked.

"If I remember correctly, I asked you first."

"Oh, yeah. You're not going to believe this. Casanova is fucking around with Charles."

"Charles?"

"Yeah, you know Charles. That's Noelle's boyfriend."

"Bitch, get out of here!" I said dramatically. But that was some real tea for my ass and I wasn't ready. I thought I was on some crazy shit, but Nova had me topped! Noelle is her damn sister. I've always known she was a scandalous bitch.

"I wish you would," Gutta mumbled.

"Shut the fuck up!" I yelled at his annoying ass.

"Now, back to you," London said.

"Nothing major. She just found out about AK and I, and shit got ugly from there."

"That's messed up. Bitches just don't be caring these days," London said, switching up the tone of her voice.

"Hell no," Gutta agreed and I looked at both of them sideways.

"Hold the fuck up now! Gutta, don't try to flex in this bitch like I haven't sucked your dick. And London, don't even try to play like you don't be fucking to get paid." I read both of their asses real quick like.

"Bitch, you ain't nothing but a hoe in my eyes. So, yeah, I let you suck my dick. So the fuck what. Better pipe the fuck down! That's why my boy gon' play ya ass to the fucking left. Don't nobody want a disloyal ass hoe like you, girl," Gutta said, and then started laughing like he had told the joke of the year.

"Damnnnnn," London said before she joined in laughing.

"Fuck y'all!" I yelled and got up. I went to AK's room and opened the door without knocking.

"Who the fuck is that?" he slurred, but didn't move.

"Are you drunk?" I asked and walked over to where he was on the bed.

"Nadia, get the fuck on. I don't want you. I miss my bitch, man," he said slow as hell. I know damn well he hadn't been over here getting drunk and upset about Harmony all of this time.

"I am your bitch. I'm here, see?" I said, trying to get him to look at me.

"I ain't talking about you, girl. I'm talking about Harmony! This shit got me fucked up!"

"Nigga, kill your fucking self!" I yelled and then slapped his ass upside the head. He groaned a little bit before hanging his head over his bed and throwing up. I nicely stepped the fuck back and made my way out of that damn apartment!

I went back to my place mad as fuck. I was hurt too, but the anger was taking over. I went to my room and lit up a blunt I had been smoking on earlier. My leg kept shaking and I had to get myself calmed down. When I was finally calm, I got up and took a shower and got dressed for work.

***

My shift at work had gone by slow as hell like it usually does. But it was finally time for me to get off, and I was happy as hell. I was past ready to go. All I wanted to do was go home, get cute and go out. I had thought about my situation with Akeem all day at work and I had come up with the plan to try to find me a new boo. That way he would be jealous and begging to get me back.

I clocked out and told the few people that were still at work, not including Carrie, bye. I made it to my car and hopped in. I tried to crank my car up, but it wouldn't crank for shit. I sat there and worked with it for 10 minutes straight before I said fuck it and decided to walk home. I lived right down the road so it wasn't that long of a walk.

When I got up by the apartments Harmony stayed in, I saw a car coming straight towards me. It was on the wrong side of the road and everything, and the lights was bright as hell. I tried to move out the way, but the car was driving down the sidewalk now. When the car slammed on the brakes, I took off running, but I only got so far before I felt something hard going across my head. I blacked out for a few minutes. When I opened my eyes, I was in a car in between two big guys in the back seat, while somebody drove us.

"What's going on? Who are you people and why the fuck did y'all hit me in the head!" I yelled.

"Nadia, I'm glad you're awake," the driver said. It was that fucking officer!

"What the fuck! Why the fuck yo' baldheaded ass got me in this damn car? Then, y'all busted me over my damn head and shit! I should fuck y'all the fuck up in this car! I swear to God y'all don't know who y'all fucking with!"

"Wild guess…a snitch?" the guy to the left of me said, and then all three of them started laughing.

"Oh, so it's funny? Y'all finding shit funny in here?! Well, it's not gone be funny when y'all laid the fuck out dead somewhere," I said, talking cash money shit.

"If anybody is going to be somewhere laid out dead," he said mocking me when he said the last part, "it's going to be you!"

I swear it felt like somebody had slapped the hell out of me when I heard him say that shit. I might have been talking all of that shit a few seconds ago, but my ass was quiet as a mouse now. I instantly started regretting all of my past actions.

I should have never slept with Akeem. I should have never crossed Harmony. I should have never snitched on Harmony. I should have just minded my fucking business and I wouldn't be in this fucked up situation. But I had to make the best out of it now.

"Look, what y'all want to know? I'll tell y'all anything. We can even go sit out in front of Harmony's place and wait for that guy. I think I might know who it is if I can see him," I rambled like a fool.

"It's too late for that! The case just got closed today. Well, the whole case isn't closed. Just hers. We can no longer watch her or bother her or we might lose our fucking jobs and it's all of your fucking fault! So, now you gotta pay," the officer said pissed.

"We can fix this. All we have to do is—" I started saying, but stopped when I felt an elbow crashing into my face. *This wasn't about to end good!*

CHAPTER 30

CASANOVA

It was finally Friday, and Mom had dragged Elle and I out shopping with her early this morning. I was tired as hell and was ready to go. Plus, I kept feeling like I had to throw up, but I kept trying to shake the feeling off. The last thing I wanted was to throw up in this damn place. It was so hot that I couldn't take being in the store anymore.

"I'm going to step outside," I said to my mom and Elle.

"Nova, no. Look, I only need to grab a few more things and then we can go, honey," my mom said before she started back shopping. Her and Elle were enjoying this shit.

Twenty minutes had passed by before we were finally at the cash register and checking out. I started feeling relieved when I saw Elle put the last bag in the buggy. My mom pulled out her wallet to pay and that's when I felt it. The throw up was coming up my throat and there was no stopping it. I ran out the store and threw up as soon as I got outside. My mom and Elle came out a few minutes later, looking at me like I was crazy.

"Nova, what's going on? Are you sick?" my mom asked as we walked to the car.

"No, Mom. I just got hot, that's all," I said and got into the car.

When we got back to Elle's home, I went straight downstairs to my room. I didn't even bother trying to help them get all of that shit for the party out of the car. It was only supposed to be us, so I don't know why they bothered getting all of that shit.

I was laid out on my bed, still feeling dizzy, when my mom came flying into my room. I sat up and looked at her with an annoyed look on my face. I wanted her here to distract Elle, not get on my last fucking nerves with her bullshit.

"What is it?" I asked.

"What do you mean? We are throwing a party tonight! I asked you if you were sick and you said no. So, get your lazy self out of that bed and come help us!" my mom said and then turned to walk out.

I didn't want to draw attention to myself for once, so I got up and moped up the stairs. I didn't need anyone finding out I was pregnant; not right now, anyway. I had plans to talk to Charles tonight though. He had been being real rude when it came to me and I was going to put a stop to that shit.

"What y'all need help with?" I asked when I walked into the living room.

"Just put your hands on something. Elle is in the kitchen cooking and I'm putting up decorations. So you can do either or." I didn't want to cook with Elle and I didn't want to smell the food she was cooking because it would probably make me sick. So, I decided to help my mom out.

When I say it took all day to set up for this so called little party, it took all day! It was almost time for the party to start by the time we finished getting everything ready. I was worn out and needed a nap, but I knew that wasn't about to happen. So, I went on downstairs and got in the shower.

I stayed in the shower for a while because it felt good to my body. Plus, I was hoping that the warm water would wake me up some, but it wasn't doing anything but making me even sleepier. I got out after I had washed up and headed to my room in my robe.

I sat on my bed to relax a little bit. When I started to feel better again, I got up and searched through my clothes. I needed to look my best tonight because 'mission get Charles' was about to go in full affect once I told him about this baby.

I settled for a little black dress that hugged my petite frame perfectly. Then, I placed a black sparkly choker around my neck to match my dress and black pumps. After I was done with that, I neatly brushed my weave up on top of my head and put it in the perfect bun. I was feeling sexy as hell and I was ready to rock this damn party.

I smoothed my dress down and made sure my stomach still looked flat in it. When I was sure it did, I headed on upstairs.

When I had got upstairs, I noticed the party had already started. Only thing is I didn't recognize most of the people in attendance. I spotted my mom and walked straight over to her.

"Who the hell are all of these people?" I asked her.

"I'm standing here trying to figure out the same thing. They all just started showing up one by one." I looked around the room and spotted Charles in the middle of the floor talking to everybody. He had a bottle of liquor in his hand and was pouring everybody up shots. He seemed to be having the time of his life. He looked over at my mom and I and smirked, before returning his attention back to the other guests. I immediately walked away from my mom in search of Noelle.

CHAPTER 31

HARMONY

It was Friday night and I was sitting in my apartment with Hazel, staring at my phone. I just kept looking at the text that Elle had sent me a few days ago. When I first saw it, I shook my head 'no' right away. I was not trying to be in the same room as Angela again. Especially not at some party she called herself having. It was going to take more than a damn party to fix our issues.

"Harmony, I wish you make up your mind so we can get going, damn," Hazel said. We had been sitting here for the last hour. We were already dressed and everything. We knew we was going out. We just didn't know where. We didn't have too many options though, because Kelly already had made it clear that he didn't want me going to no club without him.

Hazel thought he was being controlling, but I thought it was cute that he didn't want me at certain places without him. Especially since AK let me go any and everywhere without a care in the world, and he damn sure wasn't by my side. Dating Kelly had me noticing all the flaws in AK. Damn, he was one big ass joke.

"Just chill, Hazel." I said to her.

"I've been chilling for the past hour. Come on, girl! I'm trying to go somewhere. My baby gone with her grandma for the night.

My baby daddy out with his friends and I'm sitting here... with you," she said and looked at me.

"Don't do me, Hazel!" I yelled and we burst out laughing.

"I'm just saying, we might as well go to this lil' party or whatever ya mom's having. I know they got some food over there. Some drinks too, probably, and trust me, that's all I need. Plus, it's gone be free. Girl, if you don't come on!"

"Yo' ass is greedy! I guess we can go then. No need in sitting here any longer thinking about it. But, I'm telling you now. If anything happens that I don't like, I'm flipping the fuck out! I told you shit went down the other morning between my moms and I." I had told Hazel all about Angela, then I filled her in on the shit that had happened the other morning.

"Now, you know I stay ready and I'm with the shits! Let's ride!" Hazel said and stood up.

"Hell yeah! Give me a second though. I want to call Kelly right quick," I said, and then excused myself out of the living room. Kelly was out trapping so I wanted to make sure he was straight before we left. I called his phone and waited for him to answer.

"What's up, baby?" he answered and asked.

"Nothing, about to head out. I just wanted to check on you before I left."

"Hell yeah, Harmony. That's what the fuck I'm talking about. Check on yo' nigga from time to time! I like that shit, for real. But I'm straight this way. Where are you about to go?"

"I guess we gone go on over to this lil' party and see what's popping with my folks."

"Bet. Be safe. But look, I gotta go. Shoot me a text and let me know you made it when you get there."

"Alright," I said then hung up the phone. I walked back out to the living room and Hazel and I headed out.

"Kelly must be dicking you down really good now, girl," Hazel said when we were in the car.

"Why you say that?" I asked smiling. Kelly had fucked the living shit out of me the other day. Best damn dick I've ever had. After he had fucked me rough as hell, we had a round two and he slowed things down a tad bit. Everything was more sensual the second time around. I didn't think his sex game could get any better after the first round we had, but it did!

"Because look at you! Checking in with that man before you left the house. I see you, bitch!"

"You so fucking stupid, dawg. But girl, yes. Sex game on fleek!" I said and we both started cracking up once again.

We finally pulled up to Noelle's condo and got out of the car.

We knocked on the door and was let in right away by Charles. I gave him a hug, and then Hazel and I went straight to the kitchen to get something to eat and drink on.

After we had finished our food, we refilled our cups with the spiked punch and went into the living room where everybody was at. Before we could even sit down good, Elle came walking over to us.

"Mony, you made it!" she said excitedly.

"Yeah, we made it. What's up, what you doing?"

"I'm so glad, and nothing. Just making sure everybody is straight."

"Okay, well don't let me hold you up."

"No, it's fine! Who's your friend?"

"Oh, this is my home girl, Hazel."

"Hi, Hazel. I'm Elle," Elle said as she shot Hazel a friendly look.

"Hey, girl. It's good to meet you. I like yo' place. This shit right here is nice as fuck. How much you paying for rent?" Hazel asked.

"Oh, I don't know. My boyfriend pays the rent," Elle said casually.

"Damn, you got it like that? Y'all must not have no kids, huh?" Hazel asked, being nosey as fuck. I don't know what had gotten into her lately, but she was always asking questions now. I guess she done got comfortable with our friendship. That's the only thing I could think of.

"Nope, no kids. Charles and I always said we would wait a while for that. We just want to enjoy each other with no distractions."

"Ain't shit wrong with that," Hazel said smiling.

"But, Elle, check this. I got a blunt with me and I'm not trying to go outside and smoke it when I get ready for it."

"Oh, I understand. Umm, whenever you get ready, just go downstairs and smoke it and please don't pull it out up here," she said looking around.

"Thanks, sis. I got you," I said before she walked away.

The party was going smoothly and Hazel and I was on like our fifth cup of the spiked punch. I was buzzing a little bit, but that was all. That damn punch was weak as hell to me. I was used to drinking gin and shit so the punch was nothing. Hazel, on the other hand, was turnt.

"Damn, this shit boring as fuck! I might need to turn this bitch up a tad bit. Harmony, what you think?" Hazel leaned over and asked.

"Bitch, gon' head with your drunk ass," I said laughing.

"You don't never wanna have no fun, man," she pouted.

"Whatever," I said as I watched all of the people enjoy themselves.

"Harmony! How long have you been here? I didn't even see you over here," I heard someone say. I turned my head and it was Angela.

"For a lil' minute now."

"And you didn't speak?"

"Doesn't look that way."

"It sure in the fuck don't!" Hazel added in, and I had to do my best not to laugh at her drunk ass.

"Who is this… this… this PERSON?" Angela asked, frowning up at Hazel.

"This is my home girl, Hazel. Not that it's any of your business."

"Well, Hazel. You need to learn how to respect your elders. I know your mom had to teach you a thing or two when you were younger. Use it and stop acting like a hooligan in public!" Angela fussed, and I smiled because I knew Hazel was about to turn up on her ass.

"Look, woman. We not in no fucking public! We in somebody's home, and what the fuck do I look like respecting you when your own daughter doesn't even respect you? Then, you talking about use what my mama taught me. Bitch, at least she was there to teach me something, unlike your pathetic ass. So get the fuck out my face!" Hazel yelled.

"Why I never! Harmony, I want your little friend out of here!"

"I don't give a fuck about what you want, Angela," I said and rolled my eyes. She should have minded her fucking business instead of coming over here bothering me like we were cool.

"I can't believe you're going to let her talk to me this way!" Angela yelled dramatically, getting everyone's attention in the room. Hazel had already caused a few people to stop what they were doing to look at us, but now the whole room was looking. *Ahh hell!*

CHAPTER 32

PROFESSOR BLACK

I sat at the bar inside of my kitchen in deep thought. My conversation with Noelle the other day was still fresh on my mind. The way she had talked to me had pissed me off. That smug ass attitude she had over the phone didn't do anything but rub me the wrong way. She thought she had everything planned out when in reality, she didn't have a fucking clue.

She didn't have the slightest idea about the way I felt. She didn't understand how deep my love was for her. She didn't know that I dreamed about her every single night and thought about her every fucking day, even though I had tried to break shit down for her that day in my office. If that stupid ass student hadn't busted in without knocking, Noelle would be mine by now.

I wasn't able to finish talking to her. I wasn't able to finish telling her my thoughts. My desire for her had overpowered me. Just like it was doing now. I tried to shake the thoughts from my head, but it wasn't working. I grabbed the bottle of bourbon I was drinking on and poured myself another shot. If I couldn't shake the thoughts from my head, I was going to try to block them out with this alcohol.

Half an hour had passed by and the alcohol just wasn't doing it for me. That left me no choice but to do some cocaine. After I had done a couple of thick lines of the white goodness, I felt alive. I no longer wanted to shake the thoughts I was having away. Instead, I wanted to act on them. I grabbed the keys to my car and headed out of my house. Once I was inside of my car, I took off out of my driveway and down the street.

While I was driving, I came to the conclusion that Noelle's boyfriend was the problem. He was the only thing standing in my way when it came to getting her. I couldn't have that. I couldn't have him in the way of my love and I. She was destined to be with me and I was going to make that happen by eliminating the problem. *Her little boyfriend had to go!*

CHAPTER 33

NOELLE

The party had turned out a lot more packed than it was supposed to. I swear Charles invited the whole office at work. I had expected him to only invite a few people, but what I was looking at was more than a few people. I felt like a chicken with my head cut off because I was running all over the place trying to make sure everybody and everything was okay.

Nova had walked up to me a little bit after the party had started, fussing. She wanted to know who all of these people were. I told her that Charles had invited some people from work. She snobbishly looked at me before walking off. I couldn't help but to laugh at her because she was beyond pissed. Her and my mom both. But, it wasn't my fault, and there was nothing I could do about it.

I was walking through my crowded living room, overlooking everything, when I spotted Harmony. That's when I went over to talk to her. I was surprised to see her with some stranger instead of Nadia. I figured something must have been going on there that I didn't know about. Her new friend was okay; she had just asked me way too many questions. I just smiled nicely and answered them for her.

I hadn't been away from Harmony and her friend that long

when I heard a commotion coming from where they were sitting at. I eased my way through the crowd to see what was going on. When I was finally able to see, I saw Harmony's friend, Hazel, going off on my mom. Mom must have said something to piss her off because she was really letting her have it.

"What's going on over here?" I hurried up and asked because everyone was looking their way now after my mom had started flipping out.

"I want her out of here!" my mom yelled pointing at Hazel.

"Mom, just calm down," I said trying to pull her away. I would have gotten Nova to help me with her, but she had disappeared a little while ago. I figured she must be sick because she didn't look too good today. Well, she was beautiful tonight, but she must have started feeling bad again.

"I'm not going to calm down! I said I want her out of here! What is wrong with you girls?!" she yelled, and then shoved me out of the way.

"Bitch, I know you ain't just shove my sister!" Harmony jumped up and said. My mom stopped dead in her tracks and turned around to look at us.

"It's okay, Harmony. I got it," I told her before focusing on our mom. "What is wrong with us? Did you really just ask that? Did those words seriously just come out of your mouth?" I asked my mom, but then I continued to talk before she could speak. "What's wrong with us is we don't know you! Yes, we remember you, but who are you really? You waltzed yourself back into our lives and expect things to go back to normal. You expect us to just welcome you back in our lives with open arms, but that's not possible!"

"Noelle," she said firmly.

"I'M NOT FINISHED TALKING!!" I yelled.

"Damn, you tell her, boo," Mony said, watching me.

"It's not possible for us to get back to normal, and it's all your fault. I wanted to give you a chance, I really did, but I can't do that when you keep revealing who you really are. The person you really are is wicked, evil and despicable! You don't care about no one but yourself, Mom, and it's been that way for years now! Do you know how badly you affected all of us when you up and ran off? You didn't tell us bye or anything! YOU LEFT A FUCKING LETTER! A FUCKING LETTER! WHAT THE FUCK WAS YOU THINKING?!"

"My girl going off," Harmony said looking all around and smiling. I could tell she was eating this up. I wasn't done with my mother yet though.

"I sat home and blamed myself for your actions. I was young and I didn't know any better, so I blamed myself. I told myself you had left because of me. I didn't realize how ridiculous that was until my sisters talked to me about it. You have screwed us all up in more ways than one! But you had the audacity to stand there and ask what is wrong with us? YOU ARE WHAT'S WRONG WITH US!" I yelled breathing hard.

"I don't know what to say. I told you that me leaving didn't have anything to do with you girls. It was something I had to do for myself," my mom said, trying to explain herself.

"EXACTLY! YOU'RE NOTHING BUT A SELFISH BITCH!" I yelled and then stormed out of the living room. I went to my room and sat on the bed. I needed to calm down because I was pissed and I was way ahead of myself with all of the cursing. *Wait! I just called my mom a bitch!*

"Baby, are you okay?" Charles busted in the room and asked.

"I'm fine. She just pissed me off, that's all."

"Don't allow her to get you upset, beautiful. Fuck that woman! You haven't needed her this long and you still don't."

"I know. I just got upset because I was really trying with her. I wanted to give her another chance. I was willing to give her another one, Charles."

"Look, people like her don't deserve another chance, fuck her!" he said. He looked like he was about to say something else, but his phone started vibrating. He checked his message and then looked at me. "Let me go handle this," he said and then walked out of the room after he kissed me on the forehead.

I sat in my room for 30 more minutes before I went back out into the living room. When I walked out, I saw the crowd had died down some. I didn't see Charles or my mom anywhere, but Harmony was still sitting on the couch with her friend. She waved me over so I went to see what she wanted.

"Damn, Elle. You straight?" she asked.

"Yes, I'm fine."

"Good. I have never seen you turn up on somebody like that, girl."

"Yeah, I know."

"I'm glad you did though. The bitch needed to hear it. She just better be glad you stopped me because I was about to beat her ass after she shoved you like that."

"Yeah."

"But good for you, Elle. I was just making sure you were straight."

"Thanks. Where did everybody go?"

"Hell, we don't know. We been over here drinking," the girl named Hazel said.

"I'm about to go ahead and go downstairs to smoke though," Harmony said.

"Okay, that's fine," I said before she got up. I was about to see if I could find Charles until there was a knock at the door. I walked over to the door to see who was here. "Who is it?" I asked just to get no answer. I asked again, but I couldn't make out what the person was saying. So I pulled the door open to see who it was.

"Ms. Banks, I told you I would be seeing you soon," Professor Black said once I had opened the door. I tried to slam the door back shut, but it was too late. He was already making his way inside of my home. *No! No! No! He cannot be here right now!*

CHAPTER 34

HARMONY

I got up from the couch and headed down the stairs to smoke. I didn't even bother asking Hazel's ass if she wanted to come with me. She didn't smoke anyway, so there was no need for her to come with me. I didn't have time to be trying to blow my blunt smoke in the direction opposite from her.

When I got to the bottom of the steps, it was dark as hell. I tried to feel around for some lights, but I couldn't find them for shit. I made my way back over to the steps in the darkness. I figured I would just sit down on the steps and smoke, then I would head right back upstairs. Only thing is, when I tried to sit down, I ended up sitting on some fucking body.

"Ouch. Harmony, get the fuck off of me," Hazel said, slurring her words.

"Hazel, what the fuck you doing down here anyway?" I asked as I got up off of her.

"It's lame as hell up there. I wasn't about to just sit up there by myself, so I followed you down here."

"Well, you could have at least said something, damn."

"My bad. I thought you knew I was behind you."

"No, and don't be down here getting on my nerves about my blunt smoke either," I said and lit my blunt up.

"I'm chilling, man. Plus, when have I ever complained about the smoke?"

"I don't know, shit."

"You know what, I'm not even about to sit down here with your rude ass. I'm going to get me another drink," she said and stood up.

"Get me one too. I'll be back up in a few minutes."

"I might, heffa," she said and went back up the stairs.

I sat down on the steps like I was trying to do from the jump, and continued to smoke on my blunt. That shit was getting my head right too. Before I knew it, I had smoked the whole damn thing. I only intended to smoke about half of it, but once I had started hitting it, there was no putting it down until the shit was gone. I was about to try to head back upstairs when I felt my phone vibrating. I looked down and saw Kelly was calling.

"Hello?" I answered.

"What's up? You make it over there?"

"Make it over where?"

"Yo' mama house, girl," he said.

"Oh, yeah I made it."

"Yo' ass must be high."

"And you know this, man," I said and started laughing.

"You a chronic for real, baby," he said after he had stopped laughing at me.

"Lil' bit," I replied, taking his words.

"Don't be stealing my shit now."

"Shut up, ain't nobody worried about you."

"You better be. I was about to hit these streets guns blazing if you hadn't answered the phone."

"You was not."

"Yeah, aight. Why you ain't text me when you got there?"

"I did," I said, trying to think about if I had actually texted him or not. I was so high I couldn't think straight.

"Lie again."

"I really can't remember to be honest. I'm high as fuck."

"You a trip, Harmony. I'mma let you go though. I'mma try to make it back over there later, but if I don't, I'll be there in the morning. These streets booming tonight and I'm trying to take all these folks lil' money."

"Okay, bye. See you later,"

"Yeah," he said and hung up.

Once again, I was about to head up the steps, but then I heard something that didn't sound right. I made my way down the dark hall. One of the room lights was on so I went to that room since that's where the noise was coming from. When I got to the doorway, I stopped dead in my tracks. *Oh, hell no!*

CHAPTER 35

CASANOVA

If you ask me, the party was a complete waste of time. Charles had invited all of these fucking people like this was some random ass party. I brought my ass right back down the stairs. I refused to partake in that bullshit they had going on up there. I felt like they all were beneath me.

I had been down here for over an hour now, plotting and scheming on how I was going to tell Charles about the baby, and how I was going to get him down here period. That's when it came to me. I would send his ass a text. That's exactly what I did, too. In the text, I told him to bring his ass downstairs because I knew something he needed to know. Then I threatened to go upstairs and show my ass if he didn't come right away. Safe to say, he came immediately.

Now we were in the guest room. Well, we were in the master bedroom down here because I had moved into this room once I realized Charles definitely wouldn't be occupying it anymore. I was sitting on the bed in just some lingerie when he walked in. He was just standing by the door looking pissed that I had bothered him, but he knew better than to walk away from me. I had let him slide for too long with all of his slick ass comments. I bet he wouldn't say anymore slick shit after tonight.

"Charles, come sit down."

"Nova, please don't do this bullshit right now."

"Nova, please don't do this bullshit right now," I said mocking him. "Get the fuck over here! I'm sick of playing with you. Do what I say or little miss Elle will be finding out about us tonight."

"Fine, let me shut the door first."

"Fuck that door! Get over here like I said!" He held his head down and slowly walked over to the bed.

"Man, you out of line for this shit, for real. Elle and I are straight now. I know you see that shit. Whatever we had going on is over and was a big ass mistake on my end. So why don't you just get the fuck out now! I know you only moved in here to get closer to me."

"You don't know a damn thing, Charles! But, don't worry. I'm going to enlighten you on some shit very soon."

"Make it quick then. I got to get back upstairs," he said nervously, looking around.

"You seem worried, Charles," I said and then started laughing. "So, I'm a mistake now, huh? You regret what we had together?"

"Damn right!"

"Aww, I don't think you mean that. Sit," I said and patted the bed. He didn't sit though. He continued to stand like I hadn't said anything. "I SAID SIT!" I yelled. That got his ass moving. He sat down on the end of the bed. "Why are you so far away? I don't bite, remember?" I asked as I climbed down the bed towards him.

When I got to him, I started rubbing his back. Then I got up on my knees behind him and slid my hands down his chest. His body instantly relaxed. That told me that I had him. I reached further down and started rubbing on his dick through his pants. His head fell back on my chest and I smiled to myself.

"See, this isn't so bad. Don't you miss me? Don't you miss this? I know Elle isn't fucking you like I do. I know she's not. Let me give you what you have been missing, Charles." He didn't say anything, so I took that as my go ahead.

I slid off of the bed and onto the floor. Charles laid back on the bed as I got up on my knees. I undid his pants and pulled them down some. After that, I pulled his thick dick out, before taking the whole thing into my mouth. Charles immediately let out a moan. I sucked on his dick some more before I climbed on top of him.

He held my back as he slid back onto the bed. He kicked his legs until his pants and boxers were completely off. If I had of known that some smooth talking and dick sucking was all it took to get him back in my corner, I would have been done it. I knew he had to miss me because he fell for me too damn easily. Although, I am pretty hard to resist.

After his pants was off, he started kissing all on me. I started grinding my hips on top of him as I got into it. I had missed him so fucking much that just being in his arms was turning me on. I reached down and slid my panties to the side before sitting directly on his dick. It felt like a piece of heaven had entered me. I started bouncing up and down on him immediately while moaning out his name. *God, I missed this!*

Charles and I both were sweating like hell by the time we were close to our climax. I didn't care though. I just wanted to feel him nut all in me and the thought of that had me going faster and faster. We were fucking so fast and hard that the headboard was smacking the wall loud as hell. But we didn't stop. Nothing mattered to us at this moment but climaxing.

"WHAT THE FUCK?!" I heard someone yell from the doorway. But I knew that voice and it wasn't just anybody. It was Harmony. *They say what's done in the dark comes to the light, and everything was about to start coming to the light... tonight! It's game time!*

TO BE CONTINUED...

To get exclusive and advance looks at some of our top releases:

Click the link: (App Store) http://bit.ly/2hteaH7

Click the link: (google play) http://bit.ly/2h4Jw9X

Looking for a publishing home?

Royalty Publishing House, Where the Royals reside, is accepting submissions for writers in the urban fiction genre. If you're interested, submit the first 3-4 chapters with your synopsis to submissions@royaltypublishinghouse.com. Check out our website for more information: www.royaltypublishinghouse.com.

Do You Like CELEBRITY GOSSIP? Check Out QUEEN DYNASTY!

Like Our Page HERE! Visit Our Site:

www.thequeendynasty.com

CPSIA information can be obtained
at www.ICGtesting.com
Printed in the USA
LVOW10s1752210318
570660LV00014B/1039/P